Sister Joan and Brother Cuthbert had reached the boat and she stepped down into it cautiously from the slippery wooden wharf.

"I hope these old abbots didn't give you a shock." He took up the oars. "I don't mind them myself, but they are a mite creepy, I suppose. And you were actually touching one, you know."

"Don't remind me," she said. "The light went out and I was feeling along the wall for a switch and—"

"They can't hurt you, Sister." He spoke reassuringly, as if he were years older than she was. "The dead must be the most harmless creatures on earth."

"Yes, I know." She spoke sombrely, her eyes on the rippling waters as the oars parted them. The dead were indeed harmless, but the hand she had grasped in the darkness of the crypt had been warm, full-fleshed—and alive. . . .

A VOW OF SANCTITY

Veronica Black

IVY BOOKS • NEW YORK

Ivy Books
Published by Ballantine Books
Copyright © 1993 by Veronica Black

Library of Congress Catalog Card Number: 93-13349

ISBN 0-8041-1244-4

This edition published by arrangement with St. Martin's Press, Inc.

Manufactured in the United States of America

First Ballantine Books Edition: August 1994

10 9 8 7 6 5 4 3 2 1

ONE

✠ ✠ ✠

The local train, spared by the powers-that-be since it was useful for taking summer tourists where they wanted to go, chugged in a gently anachronistic manner along the side of the loch. It was September and, though the train was comparatively empty compared with the summer crowd, those who visited at this time of year were generally considered to be more discerning by the people who used the train for their weekly shopping expeditions to the nearest town. At this end of the year the gorse and heather burst into final flame before the brown tints of autumn muted the landscape.

On this particular afternoon the few passengers were mainly locals. A nun, clad in the ankle-length grey habit of her order, sat in a corner window seat and gazed out at the passing landscape with an interest that proved she was a stranger, but the women laden with shopping bags who had alighted at the last tiny station were clearly natives of the area.

The Scottish accent was really very pretty, Sister Joan was reflecting. This was the first time she had heard it in its authentic setting and the subtle differences in intonation as she had journeyed further north were interesting. As the scenery became wilder and more remote from the larger towns so the voices of her fellow travellers became softer, their pronunciation reminding her of Maggie

Smith's delicate performance in *The Prime of Miss Jean Brodie*, a film she had greatly enjoyed in the period before she had entered the religious life.

"The retreat is certainly a long way off," her prioress had remarked, "but the whole purpose of having it is to give the sister a chance to get right away from even the smallest distraction. Sometimes even the convent routine can get between ourselves and God. In silence and solitude we are enabled to look deeply into ourselves and so draw closer to Him. You will find your time there most rewarding, I'm sure."

What Mother Dorothy didn't say was that Sister Joan's absence might also be a relief for her companions. Sister Joan knew she thought it because old Sister Andrew, whose age exempted her from the obligation of being tactful, had voiced it bluntly.

"Mother Dorothy'll be glad to get rid of you for a few weeks, Sister. Do you realize that in less than a year you've twice turned the convent on its head? Now don't give me that mutinous look. Nobody denies that these matters had to be put right, but two very dramatic events in the same convent isn't the best way of attracting new vocations, is it?"

"No, Sister Andrew," Sister Joan had agreed meekly.

"Not that those of us confined to the infirmary didn't find it all rather—stimulating," the old nun added, a decided twinkle in her eyes, "but a nice quiet autumn will do us the world of good. And you will like Scotland. Have you ever visited there?"

Sister Joan shook her head.

"You must take your painting materials," Sister Andrew said. "The isles may inspire you. I visited them often when I was a girl. Walking tours with my parents. Yes, you must take time out from prayer and contemplation to paint a little."

"A retreat is not a holiday," Mother Dorothy had said severely when Sister Joan had mentioned the matter. "It is not an excuse to indulge ourselves by engaging in hobbies we enjoyed during our secular lives. On the other hand, since you do sketch and paint, and since we are enjoined not to bury our talents in the ground, I feel that you should take advantage of your stay to complete some small studies of any local beauty spot that you judge might brighten up the walls. You will not wish to sign them of course."

No Daughter of Compassion ever sought to stand out as an individual, to risk the sin of singularity. Sister Joan veiled the too eloquent blue eyes that still persisted in flying upwards from the ground and let silence imply agreement.

Going away for the month of September meant that the little school on the moor where Sister Joan taught a dozen children (the offspring of farmers who couldn't ferry their children to the nearest school bus and a handful of Romanies who refused to attend the state school regularly anyway) would have to be closed for an extra month. Sister Joan regretted that, since she enjoyed teaching and flattered herself that her pupils were doing fairly well.

"Of course Sister David could take over your duties," Mother Dorothy had said, "but she is needed for her enclosure duties and so, all things being considered, the children will have to be given an extra month's vacation. I've no doubt the local authority will have something to say about that, but I feel quite capable of dealing with any complaint they may choose to bring."

Sister Joan tried not to be too pleased at the idea that nobody could adequately replace her at the school and felt a fleeting sympathy for any member of the local education authority who tried to cross swords with little

Mother Dorothy. One glance from behind those rimless spectacles was likely to fell any officious busybody in his tracks at forty paces.

"And I said," Sister Andrew waved her off with, "that I'd make certain someone exercised Lilith while you're away."

Lilith was the placid pony on whom Sister Joan rode the distance between school and convent five days a week. Sister Joan, who had a special dispensation to wear jeans under her habit for riding, refrained from asking who would substitute for her.

The truth was, she admitted to herself during her private examination of conscience that she was spoilt. Imperceptibly she had begun to accept the small privileges, riding Lilith to school, visiting her pupils in their homes, being excused from recreation with her sisters because she had exercises to mark, as rights. She didn't believe she had neglected any of her religious duties but she sensed that the quality of her personal contribution to the life of the convent was somehow dulled by her too frequent excursions into the outer world.

"It is a pity that you will be travelling alone," Mother Dorothy observed. "I had hoped that another sister might be travelling at least part of the way but since ours is the only convent of the order in Cornwall I fear not—even the Sisters of Mercy at Bodmin aren't going anywhere this month."

The prioress who considered that Sisters of Mercy gallivanted far too often pursed up her mouth. If no Daughter of Compassion were available, her expression proclaimed, then Sister Joan was probably better off travelling alone.

"I'm sure I shall be all right, Mother Prioress," Sister Joan said mildly.

"You will break your journey overnight at Aberdeen."

"Aberdeen?" Sister Joan looked surprised. "Wouldn't it make better sense to go directly to Inverness? The retreat is on the western coast?"

"You will wish to stay with sisters of our own order and we have no convent at Inverness," Mother Dorothy said with an air of disapproval. "Then the next day you will travel westwards."

"Yes, of course, Mother Prioress."

Useless and selfish to hint that she would have preferred to break her journey at London and enjoy a brief reunion with the sisters of the convent where she had spent the testing years of her novitiate and the first years of her profession. Religious were not supposed to form particular friendships. Yet it would have been pleasant to have talked with Mother Agnes, to have spent a night under the roof where she had made the most important decisions of her life.

She was roused from her musing by a series of jerks and wheezes as the train shunted itself into another tiny wayside station. Further down one or two people got out and walked away. The train paused for a couple of minutes and then began its asthmatic choking again as the narrow platform slid away.

Sister Joan became aware of a running figure, one arm outstretched to grab at a door handle. In a moment the train would gather speed and the latecomer be flung away. She rose, stepped rapidly to the door and opened it, stumbling back as the would-be passenger took a flying leap into the middle of the compartment. For a moment the open door swung wildly; then he leaned to slam it, sat down in the nearest seat and turned a freckled, ingenuous countenance towards her.

"God bless you for that, Sister. If I'd missed the train Father Abbot'd have murdered me."

"Not literally I hope, Brother—?" Sister Joan resumed her original seat and raised her eyebrows enquiringly at the young monk.

"Cuthbert," he supplied.

"Cuthbert."

Why Cuthbert, for heaven's sake? Cuthbert might have been a great hunter whose conversion to Christianity came about when he saw the Christ impaled on the antlers of a deer he was chasing but the name had acquired down through the centuries a definite quality of wimpishness. Perhaps the abbot had wished it on the young man. In any case it was none of her business.

"Father Abbot," Brother Cuthbert was saying feelingly, "can be quick tempered, though not, of course, to the point of murder. Are you going to the retreat, Sister—?"

It was his turn to look enquiring.

"Sister Joan. Yes, I am. You know it?" She felt a flutter of interest.

"One of my duties is to keep it swept and clean in between visits from the sisters," he informed her. "Of course nobody intrudes when a sister is there, though if she's taken ill or any emergency arises we're near enough to give help."

"I do not intend," said the prioress at the Aberdeen convent in an irritatingly coy manner, "to tell you anything about our retreat. It ought to come as a surprise."

That had been said during recreation the previous evening. Sister Joan had been welcomed warmly by the community, and had felt adequately compensated for not having stayed over at her old convent, but the remark had jarred on her.

"It is on Loch Morag, isn't it?" she had said in reply, her own tone severely practical.

"In a very beautiful situation," the prioress had said, "but you will see for yourself. My only regret is that more of our order don't take advantage of its existence regularly. In the early days just after the war there was always one sister or other staying there, but there hasn't been anyone there for over a year."

Sister Joan, who had envisaged herself embarking on a thorough spring clean before she got down to any spiritual exercises, gave Brother Cuthbert a kindly look.

"I have instructions as to how to reach the retreat," she said, "but it is very reassuring to meet someone who actually takes care of the place. Will there be supplies there? Food and so on?"

"They can be brought in fast enough," Brother Cuthbert told her. "I can make sure that you have supper tonight anyway and then tomorrow I'll bring what you'll be needing over the next few days. We're coming into the station now. Give me your bags, Sister. The train only stops for a moment."

He was already on his feet, shouldering her bags, reaching for the door. A powerfully built young man, she judged, who looked as if rugger had been his game at school. His freckled face was surmounted by a tonsured crown of ginger hair and the general impression he gave was one of wide-eyed enthusiasm.

"Mind how you go, Sister." He turned as he alighted to give her a helping hand down to the narrow wooden walkway that served as platform.

"Thank you." Sister Joan, refraining from the comment that she was thirty-six and not yet in her dotage, stepped down and looked round as the train with an air of having shrugged off its cargo chuntered out again, Brother Cuthbert reaching out a long arm to slam the door.

A wooden barrier behind which a hill dotted with small houses and lined with narrow, twisting lanes, denoted the limits of the tiny station.

"That's the village on the slope of the hill," Brother

Cuthbert said helpfully. "We're largely self-supporting in the community but occasionally we do a spot of shopping there. We go this way."

He shouldered her bags again as if they were filled with tissue paper and strode through a gap in the wooden barrier. At the other side a road snaked around the base of the hill on which the village was perched.

"We take the bridge over the railway," Brother Cuthbert said over his shoulder. "Then you'll see the loch proper. Our community is on a kind of spur of land that juts out into the loch. The retreat is on the hill above. There are steps cut in case you have weak legs."

"I think mine are fairly sturdy," Sister Joan assured him.

"It's no more than a twenty-minute walk," Brother Cuthbert said cheerfully. He had already outstripped her. Sister Joan put on a little spurt in order to keep her luggage within sight.

They had reached the steel girders of the bridge that provided access to the other side of the single gauge line. At the far end the steps descended to a narrow gully below which the beginning of the loch threaded itself between heather clad slopes. Over in the west where she could see the sparkle of wider water, the late afternoon splashed glory across the sky.

"You'll admit it's a good view," Brother Cuthbert said, stopping abruptly. Sister Joan nodded without speaking. Beauty sometimes had that effect, she thought, of rendering any comment superfluous, of catching at the heart.

"Yes, well." Brother Cuthbert shot her a vaguely disappointed glance. He had probably expected more verbal enthusiasm. "We go through this gully to the shores of the loch and then you'll see the path and the steps up to the retreat."

He strode across the narrow track and entered a gully that provided an access to the other side of the slope. Following him, Sister Joan looked up at massive walls of rock scarred by deep fissures. It was impossible to tell if the gully was man-made or the result of some cataclysm of nature. Either way it struck her as deeply impressive. At the foot of the cliffs boulders were scattered around, some sunken into the ground, half covered with lichen.

"Loch Morag," said Brother Cuthbert, turning as they reached the other end of the gully.

"And it's magnificent," Sister Joan breathed. The shores of the loch lay below her, reed and iris fringed with a scattering of willows leaning over the shallow banks. At the opposite shore the cliffs rose sheer to the rose and orange and gold of the afternoon sky.

"Actually it rains quite a bit," Brother Cuthbert admitted. "The weather here can change drastically in about twenty minutes. That's partly why the community was founded in the beginning—to help travellers who got lost when the mist and the rain came down. In the ninth century, that was when the Vikings were sailing along these coasts, they say the retreat was originally a look-out post where one of the monks could keep watch for any sight of a dragon ship. Some of the Vikings settled further inland. Oh, you'll be wanting to get to your destination. You see the path? If you follow that you reach the retreat. You can't see it from this angle."

He indicated the steep slopes behind them, where conifers clung to the earth below the higher peaks of rock and a path snaked between the trunks.

"Right then." Sister Joan tore her gaze away from the scenery and reached out for her bags.

"You'll never manage both of them, Sister," Brother Cuthbert said firmly. "Look, you take the lighter one

and I'll bring up the heavier with something for your
supper just as soon as I've seen Father Abbot. Give me
half an hour."

"You said your community was on a spur of land,"
Sister Joan said, looking across the glinting surface of
the loch.

"Around the bend just past that outcropping of rock,"
he pointed. "It is possible to walk across the stepping
stones when the water's calm but there is a boat we can
use when we need to leave the enclosure. Are you sure
you can cope with a bag? I can bring over the both if
not."

"I'll manage just fine," Sister Joan assured him.

"Right then—see you later, Sister. Take care now."

He had relinquished the lighter of her bags and now
strode off along the fringed shoreline, still carrying the
heavier one. Under the hem of his brown habit his sandalled feet trod rapidly. It was obvious that punctuality
was considered important. She turned back towards the
cliff path and began to mount it, pleased to find that it
was easily negotiable.

It twisted back and forth between the trees, doubling
back on itself at times, the gradient becoming almost
imperceptibly steeper so that with a little shock she
paused to catch her breath, suddenly aware that her feet
were slipping on the sharp pine needles that littered the
ground and that the shores of the loch were a long way
below her. She set down her carpetbag on a bit of level
ground and looked down through the trees to where the
cliffs seemed to converge, the loch itself narrowing to a
ribbon of glinting silver. From this height it was possible to see the spur of land that jutted out from the opposite shore to form what amounted to a virtual island
where the loch widened again, as it emerged from the
outcroppings of rock and pine-clad slope below the

scree and jagged peaks above the tree-line. She could see trees on the spur and the straight lines of stone walls and what could have been low stone buildings, but it was all too distant to make out in any detail. And it had nothing to do with her anyway save that it was pleasant to know that in an emergency she wouldn't be completely alone.

"And there is not," said Sister Joan aloud, "going to be any emergency, so let's go on."

She bent, picked up her bag, and toiled on up the steepening path. If any elderly Daughter of Compassion wished to make a spiritual retreat, she reflected wryly, she'd do well to have a medical checkup first.

The path had ended abruptly in what looked like a solid face of rock. She stared upward in dismay for a moment. Then she saw the steps—broad, shallow steps cut in the stone and rising upwards with an iron handrail on the side furthest from the rock.

The steps twisted as they neared the top and ended at what reminded her of an illustration that had been in her childhood copy of *The Piper of Hamelin*. A door fixed in the mountainside would doubtless open to reveal the enchanted land beyond. Putting down her bag on the top step, Sister Joan lifted the huge iron latch with the same stir of excitement as the child Joan had once looked at the picture in her book, and stepped into a narrow passage—no more than a cleft in the rock.

Within a couple of yards it widened into a cave, fairly spacious and with a reasonably level floor. She held her bag in front of her and manoeuvred it and her own slight frame into the larger space. Even with the door open it was dim after the sunlit landscape below but not uncomfortably dark. More light filtered through a slit in the rock. Again it was impossible to tell if it were man-made or natural, but it clearly served as a window. Stepping to it, Sister Joan looked out, first seeing only sky, and then as she shifted her head, watching the sweep of the loch as it wended its way, the open sea came into view. A look-out post for Vikings, she reminded herself, and felt a curious kinship with the long dead monks who had taken their turn as look-out scouts, anxiously straining their gaze towards the sea, dreading the sight of a carved dragon prow breasting the waves.

The cave was simply furnished. An iron bedstead with mattress and blankets—how, she wondered, had they managed to get it up the steps?—a primus stove, a shelf with some dishes and cups and cutlery ranged along it, a few hooks hammered into the wall, and at the back of the cave a shallow stone trough which formed a natural washbasin. There were also half a dozen large plastic containers of water which looked fresh and fit for drinking. Presumably Brother Cuthbert renewed the contents regularly. She bent to unscrew the lid, dipped a cup into the wide neck and was rewarded with a welcome, thirst-quenching draught of cool water.

"Much healthier than a cup of tea," Sister Joan admonished herself, and grinned as she realized she had spoken aloud. Five minutes in the retreat and she was talking to herself!

She had carried up the lighter bag containing her nightclothes and change of underwear and toilet accessories. Brother Cuthbert had gone off with the bag containing her painting materials and the thick notebook in which she wrote up her meditations. Entries, she thought guiltily, had been sparse in recent months, but the schoolday took up so much of her time, demanded so much emotional energy—and there she went making excuses again. Mother Dorothy had known what she was talking about when she recommended a period of spiritual renewal.

She stepped into the narrow passage again and went through the doorway to the broad, flat top step. Wider than the other steps it had a guard rail about it, a sensible modern precaution of which she heartily approved. She herself had an excellent head for heights but in wet weather the stone would be slippery and the cliffs were steep.

From the top step she had a splendid view of the length of the loch as it curved into wider water and of the spur of land that jutted into it with its trees and long lines of grey stone wall. Colours were muted in this distance and only the sky flashed fire. There was a boat on the loch. She narrowed her eyes to bring it into focus and guessed rather than saw that Brother Cuthbert was on his way with her other bag and, hopefully, something for supper. Sister Joan whose trim figure belied a hearty appetite trusted that the young Brother hadn't picked up the notion that a retreat also meant extremes of fasting.

"In the Order of the Daughters of Compassion extremes of devotion are not encouraged," her first prioress had said. "Excessive self-mortification is dangerous and silly. Please remember that."

Sister Joan had never had any idea of doing anything to excess, but now as she watched the boatman draw towards the shore she felt another uneasy pang of guilt. So far she had admired the scenery, thought cravingly of a cup of tea, and hoped she'd get a decent supper, and not one prayer of thankfulness for a safe journey had come into her head.

Brother Cuthbert had moored the boat and was striding along the water's edge with her larger bag in one hand and what looked like a picnic hamper in the other. He began to mount the lower path between the trees with the sure-footedness of a goat. Clearly he would ascend the steps with equal ease, not needing to hold on to the handrail. Sister Joan stepped back as his fringe of ginger hair appeared directly beneath her and retreated into the cave, leaving the door open.

"Glad you're settled in, Sister." He had inserted himself and his burdens through the narrow passage. "Quite a climb, isn't it? Oh, Father Abbot just had the letter from your own convent to let us know someone was coming on retreat. The post never comes on time here."

"I'm surprised it ever arrives at all," Sister Joan said frankly. "It is pretty remote."

"The local postmistress comes on her bicycle," Brother Cuthbert explained, setting down his load, "and puts any letters for our community into a postbox on the near shore. Father Abbot has the largest post bag, quite a regular series of communications with lay workers in the field."

"The field?" Sister Joan glanced at him enquiringly.

"The mission field," Brother Cuthbert said. "We are the contemplative part of our Order but we have brothers and secular workers in the Third World. It is prayer that helps them to continue."

"And a few financial contributions," Sister Joan reminded him. Brother Cuthbert looked unhappy.

"One wishes money wasn't so important," he said.

"Money is very useful provided it's earned and spent in the same way," Sister Joan said with spirit. "Wasn't it Saint Teresa of Avila who said that with God she could do a lot but with God and some ducats she could do more?"

"Yes, of course. How right you are to remind me that practical things matter too," he said with the swift contrition of someone to whom the religious life was clearly still very new and shining.

She would have liked to ask him why he had felt drawn to the contemplative side of his order rather than to more physically demanding missionary work, but Brother Cuthbert's reasons for doing anything at all were none of her business, so she contented herself with an inarticulate murmur and bent to the wicker basket he had placed on the floor.

"Shall I empty this, Brother Cuthbert? You'll need to take it back?"

He shook his head. "You can bring it over yourself, Sister, when you come to mass," he told her.

"I was going to ask you about that. The local church . . . ?"

"Is called a kirk and is Protestant. There is a chapel in our own community where the few Catholics around come to mass on holy days. Father Abbot offers the mass at ten in the morning on Sundays and feast days. For the community he offers it every day, of course."

"Do I use the boat?" she enquired.

"The parishioners have their own small fishing boats they use as transport, but I bring the craft to this side of the loch for anyone who needs it."

"Fine. I'll see you the day after tomorrow then."

"If there should be any emergency," he said, "there's a bell you can ring."

"Where?" She looked around.

"Just outside the look-out post. If you put your hand through the gap you can feel the end of the rope. If you need help you ring the bell and it sounds right across the loch."

Sister Joan smiled somewhat doubtfully. It occurred to her that an accident was more likely to happen when one was on the steps outside than inside the retreat in which case it might prove impossible to tug at the rope.

Perhaps the bell was there to provide psychological security.

"Enjoy your supper, Sister." Brother Cuthbert gave her a smiling nod and prepared to depart, his sandalled feet plodding rapidly through the door and down the stone staircase to the path below.

The wicker hamper contained rolls that had clearly been freshly baked that day, a slab of yellow cheese, a jar of herrings in vinegar, a small box of tea bags, several boxes of matches, a small jar of cooking oil, a packet of digestive biscuits, and a few onions and apples. At the bottom of the hamper a crock of honey and a couple of saucepans completed what were evidently regarded as desirable for a nun on a spiritual retreat to consume.

"And God bless you for the tea bags," Sister Joan breathed after the tiny figure now loping along the shore.

She half filled one of the saucepans with water from the plastic containers and knelt down to light the primus stove, feeling as if she had been catapulted back into a camping trip she'd gone on with a school party when she was fourteen.

A lamp with wick ready trimmed hung on a hook from an area where the cave roof slanted lower. With the last of the sunset vanishing the cave itself was becoming very dim. Nevertheless it seemed warm and dry enough and she certainly seemed to be supplied with necessities. Except for a lavatory.

While the water was heating she squeezed her way past an overhanging curtain of rock to the far end of the cave where a discreetly sited chemical toilet was hidden from the main living area. Brother Cuthbert had obviously been too bashful to direct her to it personally. Its existence was cheering. While the notion of a month-long spiritual retreat might have had a medieval flavour it was reassuring to find modern aids to hygiene and cleanliness.

The tea was strong, hot and sugarless. Sister Joan sat on an outcropping of rock that did duty for a stool and drank it gratefully. A roll and cheese with some sliced onion would do very nicely for her supper, but first she would finish her unpacking and then light a couple of the candles she had brought. Kindling the heaven-pointing flames and setting them in their tin holders on a low ledge she felt the tiredness after a long journey begin to slip away.

She laid her Prayer Book between the candles, knelt down and began her prayers. In the convent, supper would now be served and one of the sisters would be reading aloud from a devotional book—the life of Margaret Clitheroe, Sister Joan reminded herself, with its graphic account of the saint's martyrdom guaranteed to put anyone off their food. She bit her lip as the irreverent thought popped into her mind.

"Humour is a splendid attribute to possess," Mother Dorothy had recently remarked, "provided that it is not indulged in at inappropriate times."

She hadn't looked at anybody in particular as she made the remark but Sister Joan had felt the tip of the arrow just the same.

She detached her rosary beads from her belt and began the murmured recitation of the mysteries. Her stomach growled a little, reminding her that she hadn't yet eaten, and she resisted the temptation to gabble to a close. The candles she had lit burned with a steady fire in the darkening cave. Above the whispered cadences of her own voice the wind rose, its shriek having in it something primeval as it whistled over the high peaks and fell into the valley in a cascade of dying echoes.

"Amen," said Sister Joan, and rose.

She would brew herself another cup of tea and eat the supper she had decided upon. Then she would clean her teeth, extinguish the candles, and grope her way to the iron-railed bunk with its thin mattress and coarse blankets.

The cheese was strong tasting and buttery, the roll satisfyingly crisp. She drank the second cup of tea but it tasted bitter now that her immediate thirst had been quenched. She would find out if it was possible to buy milk from the monks when she went over to mass on the Sunday.

The door had a bolt on the inside which she hadn't yet fastened, though it was hardly likely that anyone unauthorized would come visiting her in the middle of the night. Nevertheless she went to the door and, after a moment's hesitation opened it and stepped cautiously outside. An overhanging lintel of stone protected her from the wind and she stood in an oasis of calm, her gaze turning to the dark bulk of the cliffs under a sky wreathed now with night over a landscape from which all colour had fled.

Someone was moving along the shore of the loch. She heard from far down the pitter patter of iron-shod hoofs against pebble and saw in a brief glance the rider and steed, foreshortened by distance, between two clumps of pine.

A woman to judge from the long hair that had streamed behind her. Sister Joan had glimpsed no more than that before the tossing branches of the trees and the rapidly encroaching dark hid rider and horse from view. Then she stepped back within the door, closing it, sliding the bolt home. On this first night, she decided, she would leave the candles burning.

TWO

✠ ✠ ✠

Six years of convent life had accustomed Sister Joan to
dawn rising. A subdued grey light filtered through the
lookout window and there was a fresh breeze. Habit got
her out of bed and on her knees with the traditional
"Christ is risen," usually spoken by the lay sister who
came round to waken the fully professed.

"Thanks be to God," she answered herself and rose,
resisting the impulse to crawl back under the blankets
for an extra half hour.

Cleaning one's teeth, washing and dressing in a cave
had a certain novelty value, she reflected. There were
communal retreats held from time to time, usually on
some particular theme, but a solitary retreat demanded
more both physically and mentally. That one's living
space should be hollowed out of rock put one in tune
with the hundreds of contemplatives down through the
centuries who had sought God in silence and solitude.

She glanced at the neat fob watch pinned to her belt
and saw it was not yet six. The most sensible course of
action would be to tidy up the interior and then sit
down and make a timetable for herself. Otherwise she
was likely to spend too much time admiring the scenery
and planning to pray for a longer period the day after.
Sister Joan who was more clearheaded about herself

than Mother Dorothy credited performed the few necessary chores and sat down with her notebook.

5 a.m.	— Rise. Two hours prayer and contempla-tion.
7 a.m.	— Breakfast. Clean retreat.
8 a.m.	— Walk.
10 a.m.	— Paint.
1 p.m.	— Lunch.
1.30 p.m.	— Spiritual reading and exercises.
4.30 p.m.	— Tea.
5 p.m.	— Exercise.
6.30 p.m.	— Examination of conscience and evening prayers.
8 p.m.	— Supper and bed.

And let's hope, she thought, regarding her itinerary,
that I can keep all my own rules.

Sundays would be different with mass to attend in the
monastery chapel and possibly a Benediction later in
the day. This morning she would need to walk over to
the village for a few supplies since it wasn't fair to expect the monks to supply everything. Frowning slightly
she turned over the page and began on a shopping list.

In the convent the lay sisters did the shopping as a
rule though the fully professed were not strictly enclosed. Those who were obliged to earn a living beyond
the enclosure had dispensation to do so. But living in a
convent did to a certain extent cocoon one from the re-
alities of everyday living. In six years of convent life
Sister Joan hadn't had to worry about paying rent or
mortgage or budgeting for a week's groceries.

She would need some flour—pancakes would be simple enough to make—eggs, a jar of coffee, a couple of
lemons, some tuna fish—tin opener, since there wasn't

one here—milk until she found out if the monks kept a
cow. Butter? Margarine. She wrote it down and chewed
the end of her pencil. What on earth did one buy for
oneself? Her order forbade the eating of meat save at
Christmas and on Easter Day, but cheese, fish, fruit, and
vegetables were consumed in a variety of tasty dishes.

"Fruit gums," she said aloud and wrote down the
item.

"A tiny treat now and then is very good for the soul,"
Sister Andrew had remarked during one of their chats.

Sister Andrew was in her eighties and entitled to occasional treats. Sister Joan wasn't at all sure that she
merited the same but she let the two words stand and
carefully detached the page from the notebook. It was
an extremely modest shopping list to which she would
probably add when she got to the shops. Meanwhile she
had better get on her knees and do a little praying.

At 8.30, her prayers having lengthened into a full-
blown meditation that took no account of timetables,
Sister Joan emerged from the retreat and looked out
over the loch. The sun was still only a pale disk in the
sky but the breeze had the gentleness of spring rather
than autumn. The screaming wind of the previous night
had died away and the surface of the loch was only
slightly ruffled by little, dancing waves. She closed the
heavy door behind her and went cautiously down the
steps, holding the guard rail. It wasn't impossibly steep
though she reckoned it would be tricky in wet or snowy
conditions. On the other hand no prioress in her senses
would permit one of her nuns to come to this remote retreat in the depths of winter.

She gained the lower slopes without difficulty and
paused to get her bearings. Further along this ridge of
high cliffs was the gully that cut through to the parallel
track with the single gauge railway line beyond the

bridge and the village sprawling over the slopes. There would be shops there, perhaps a Saturday market. She retraced the route along which Brother Cuthbert had guided her the previous day, not hurrying since she had allowed plenty of time for a walk. This morning the shoreline was deserted. No woman with long, flowing hair galloped a horse along the shingle.

She cut through the gully and walked towards the scatter of houses clinging to the slopes of the next range of hills. Close to she could see that the narrow, twisting lanes between the buildings were cobbled, the houses themselves built of granite-dark stone with roofs of sombre slate, almost every dwelling having between front door and lane a small yard, incongruously bright with vivid flowers in tubs or growing along the tops of low dividing walls.

She slowed her step, aware that her arrival had been instantly remarked. Not a soul came out to stare but she was conscious of the twitching of a curtain here, the part opening of a door there, a heightening of tension impossible to pinpoint but unmistakable. She walked more slowly, glancing about her. A small boy who had been swinging on a gate jumped down as she neared him, alarm in his face, his thumb and little finger shooting out from his clenched fist in the age old sign of protection against the evil eye.

Sister Joan repressed a sigh. She had forgotten that in certain communities nuns were regarded as harbingers of bad luck, living omens to be avoided or jeered at. Brother Cuthbert had said there were few Catholics in the district but he had not mentioned there might be prejudice. Well, the only way to combat prejudice was to try to ignore it. She raised her chin in the manner her father had always called "Our Joan's bulldog look," and spoke clearly and pleasantly.

"Good morning. I need some groceries. Can you tell me where the grocer's shop is?"

The small boy stared at her wordlessly. At the same moment the door behind him opened suddenly and a voice called sharply, "Come away in, Dougal!"

"Are you Dougal's mother?" Sister Joan stepped briskly to the gate. "I'm hoping to buy some groceries. If you would be so kind as to direct me to the shops?"

"The store's at the top of the hill."

The owner of the voice had come to the open door and ventured as far as the front step. Sister Joan smiled across the yard at the thin young woman with her hair tied severely back and her garments covered by a large apron.

"Thank you. That's very kind of you. I'm Sister Joan—"

"We don't hold with being converted here," the young woman interrupted.

"I'm not in the business of conversion," Sister Joan said mildly. "Good day to you."

She turned and went on up the cobbled hill. Behind Dougal's voice was raised shrilly.

"Is she a witch, Mam? Is she?"

The answer was inaudible. Dougal had evidently been yanked indoors.

A double-fronted store which obviously sold a wide range of goods occupied a large corner building at the top of the hill. Sister Joan paused to look at the plate-glass windows crammed with merchandise. A couple of women emerging with laden baskets glanced at her curiously.

Where, she thought wryly, was the traditional friendliness the travel brochures always talked about when they advertised the Highlands? Perhaps if she had not been clad in ankle-length grey habit and short veil over a white coif that hid her short dark hair people would have nodded and greeted her in the soft accent that was so attractive.

She entered the store which was as crowded with wares as the windows, sacks of potatoes vying with plastic pots of yoghurt and some brightly jacketed paperback books sharing a revolving stand with picture postcards depicting views of the loch. Towards the back of the store a long open-ended counter was presided over by a middle-aged woman who gave her a slightly startled look, then moved forward.

"Ah, you'll be come to stay up at the hermitage," she said.

"At the retreat, yes."

"Not often anyone comes there these days. Out of fashion, I daresay. I'm Dolly McKensie."

"Sister Joan." Shaking hands Sister Joan added, "You're not from this area?"

"Carlisle, and why I ever left I'll never know. Must have been meeting my late husband. Born and bred at Loch Morag he was and we spent our married life here until—but what can I get you, Sister?"

Here at least was someone who seemed friendly enough. Sister Joan handed over her list and watched Mrs. McKensie run her eye down it.

"I can supply all this, Sister," she said obligingly. "Were you wanting potatoes? The monks grow sufficient for their own needs, but it'd be better for you to take a small sackful from me. I can send Rory over with the lot as soon as he gets in."

"Your husband?"

"My son. My husband—he's been gone nearly six years now."

"I'm sorry."

Sister Joan's hand rose to trace a cross just as Dolly

McKensie said vigorously, "Oh, he's not dead, Sister. No such luck for me! He ran off nearly six years ago and nobody's seen hide nor hair of him since. Not that he was the best husband in the world when he was around but still it's hard to bring up a lad without a father. Rory turned out well though. I'm proud of him."

"I'm sure you are," Sister Joan said warmly, adding, "perhaps it would be a good idea to buy some potatoes from you. The brothers have been very generous but I don't want to take advantage of them."

"I'll have Rory bring the lot up," Dolly McKensie said. "Was there anything else you wanted while you were here, Sister?"

"Nothing, thank you. You've been very helpful," Sister Joan said.

"You'll not find many so friendly in these parts," a voice said from the doorway. "We don't take to outlanders hereabouts as a rule, especially if they're Catholics."

Turning, Sister Joan looked up at a tall, raw-boned young man whose reddish hair and long upper lip betokened the Celt.

"Outlanders?" she queried.

"Anyone not born in Loch Morag," the newcomer said.

"Sister Joan is come to buy some groceries for herself," Dolly said. "This is my son, Rory, Sister."

No more than twenty, Sister Joan reckoned, shaking hands. He had grey eyes beneath shaggy brows and a fresh complexion with a faint stubble along the jaw.

"Groceries?" The shaggy brows lifted. "I thought you'd be fasting."

"Only on Fridays and on Tuesdays when the moon is full," Sister Joan said solemnly. "Why don't people like

Catholics and what are outlanders supposed to do to get accepted into the community?"

"They don't." He answered her last question first with a slight lifting of the lips that might have passed for a smile. "Why, my mother's been here for more than twenty years and she's still regarded as an immigrant."

"And you're not Catholic?"

The smile darkened into a scowl. "We are not," Rory said curtly.

"But you don't mind serving them. That's a relief."

"We like to make a profit," Rory said in the same curt tone. "We don't give credit either."

"I wasn't asking," Sister Joan said mildly, bringing out her purse.

"And it's twenty-five pence extra for deliveries," he added, ignoring his mother's embarrassed frown.

"Fine," Sister Joan said. "I'll pay you when I see the goods outside the door of the retreat. Thank you, Mrs. McKensie. I'm obliged to you. Mr. McKensie."

She nodded coolly and went out into the street again. Behind her, just before the door closed, she heard Dolly McKensie say angrily, "Will you never learn to behave like a civilized being, Rory? Is it her fault now that she's a Papist?"

Papist! Sister Joan's lips twitched as she walked down the hill. She hadn't realized that the old term of insult was still used anywhere. Papist sounded vaguely threatening, bringing with it memories buried deep in the racial subconscious—the smashing of stained-glass windows and the execution of priests at Tyburn and the martyrdom of Margaret Clitheroe at York. Ancient times with a legacy of bitterness best forgotten.

Someone threw a stone.

It missed her, bouncing sharply on the cobbles as she swung round in time to see a towhead duck behind the nearest wall. Dougal's house, Sister Joan thought, remembering the young woman's anxious cry of "Come away in."

She hesitated, not wanting to make more of the incident than it warranted, but feeling a distinct disinclination to turn the other cheek.

"You come out here, Dougal Mackintosh!"

A voice that echoed her own suppressed wrath bellowed down the narrow street as Rory McKensie strode down past her, leaned over the wall, and hauled up the child by the lapels of his jacket, dangling him in the air threateningly.

"I didna mean no harm," Dougal piped, looking less terrified than Sister Joan would have felt in the same situation.

"Don't you know that the sister here has the power to turn you into a frog?" Rory demanded.

"Oh no I haven't," Sister Joan said coldly. "And if I had I wouldn't try to improve on nature!"

"Behave yourself or I'll hand you over to the brothers," Rory said grimly, letting the child drop.

Dougal, released, uttered a shrill cry and fled within the safety of his gate.

"You had no business to say such a thing," Sister Joan scolded. "How can we ever have mutual toleration and forgiveness if you go putting ideas into the child's head?"

"Your own remark wasn't all sweetness and light," Rory commented, picking up a large sack which he had deposited in the road and hunching it over his shoulder as he fell into step beside her.

"My besetting sin," she admitted, "is a too ready tongue. The Lord knows what dreadful trauma I've caused the poor child."

"Dougal Mackintosh," said Rory calmly, "will be all

the better for a trauma or two. He's growing up into a hooligan. Since I'm here I'll walk along with you."

"Those are the groceries?" Sister Joan eyed the sack in surprise.

"My mother added a few extra," Rory said, suddenly looking embarrassed.

"That was very kind of her." Sister Joan found it difficult to keep the surprise out of her voice. "Are you— you're not Catholic, you said?"

"Meaning that only Catholics do good turns for other people?" The hostility was back.

"Meaning that Catholics don't seem to be too popular round here."

"This is John Knox territory," Rory said. "The kirk and very boring Sundays and if you're enjoying yourself then there's sin in it."

"We have our puritan side too. So you're . . .?"

"My father was a Catholic," Rory said. "I was brought up as one but I lost my faith when—I lost it."

They had left the village and were crossing to where the gully ran between the high rocks. Sister Joan refrained from comment and after a moment or two Rory said defensively, "You haven't said anything about praying for me."

"It always sounds a bit patronizing and pious to go round threatening prayer," she said mildly. "Of course I probably will, sooner or later. But that needn't worry you too much."

"I won't let it," Rory said sharply.

"Good." Sister Joan grinned at him amiably.

"My mother isn't Catholic," Rory said, imparting further information as reluctantly as if she had asked for it. "It was a mixed marriage, but I was reared as a Catholic. I stuck to it until—well, one outgrows it, you know."

"I'm afraid I'm retarded then," Sister Joan said apologetically.

Rory uttered a shout of laughter which he turned hastily into a cough. He was still very young, she thought, and felt a twinge of amused compassion. Young men leaping out of boyhood reminded her of colts trying to jump a high fence.

"What beats me," Rory said as they began the climb up the slope, "is why someone like you should ever enter a convent. I mean, you're still quite young, aren't you?"

"You think I ought to have waited until I was drawing my old-age pension?" Sister Joan paused to catch her breath. "What an odd idea of nuns you have. And you a cradle Catholic too!"

"Now you're making fun of me."

"A little bit," she confessed. "However you are being slightly impertinent, don't you think? My reasons for choosing the religious life are private."

"A failed love affair? If so, then I apologize for upsetting you," he said stiffly.

Sister Joan's vividly blue eyes misted over with the memory of forgotten dreams. No, she and Jacob had not failed. Only the barrier between them had grown too high for either of them to breach. Jacob had reverted in the end to his Jewish heritage and she had found it impossible to give up her Christian one. But that, she reflected, hadn't been the real reason why she had chosen the religious life. It had merely provided the particular circumstances in which she had begun to think seriously about it. The real reason was love, she suspected. A greater love seeking a lesser love in order to experience itself.

"If you think I'm about to provide you with my life story, forget it," she said crisply.

"Meanie." He gave her the grin that he must have worn as a schoolboy.

They had reached the steps and he stood aside to let her go first.

"Oh, I can be terribly mean," Sister Joan assured him. "D'ye need a hand with the sack? It looks heavy."

"My mother put in a lot of tinned stuff," he told her. "She has a kind of liking for Catholics."

"Well, she married one."

The remark, innocently meant, brought a flush of anger to his face, and the gaze he turned upon her was a stormy one.

"She's told you then? About my father, I mean? She often mentions it to strangers as if she's hoping that one day someone will say, 'Wait a moment! I met the man that you're describing only last week.' She still thinks that he might come back one day. Not that she'd admit it to me."

"You don't want your father to come back?" Sister Joan opened the door and went through the narrow entrance into the cave. Behind her Rory was pulling the sack through after him.

"No I don't." He stood straighter, the sack at his feet. "We get on very well without him, Mum and I. He was always wandering off anyway—sales representative when he should have been taking some of the load off my mother's back and helping her run the shop. Then one weekend he simply didn't come home. We waited a couple of weeks and then Mum went to the police."

"She didn't go immediately?"

"He often stayed away for days but never for a fortnight before. Anyway she didn't get much change out of the local Constabulary. They made some enquiries in case he'd had an accident but nothing turned up. They did find out that he'd given up his job a few days before he left. But they never found him or his car. Mum was upset."

"And you?" Sister Joan asked as casually as she could.

"I was fourteen already and not a silly kid." He shrugged his shoulders in a disparaging fashion. "We were never close anyway—my father and I, I mean. Not that I was a mother's boy if that's what you're thinking."

"I wasn't," Sister Joan said. She judged it unnecessary to let him know that she had noticed the time when his father had decamped had coincided with his loss of faith.

"Delivery," he said, with an air of changing the subject, "is extra."

"And cheap when one considers the effort involved." She dug in her purse and found the coins. "Please thank your mother for the extras. It was very kind of her."

"I'd better be off then." He bent slightly beneath the rough stone lintel, and turned to face her again as they stepped outside. "Look, I don't hold any brief for the pious brigade but if there's anything else you want . . .?"

"Thanks but I'll be fine," Sister Joan began, then hesitated. "There is one thing, probably not important. Is there anyone around here who rides along the shores of the loch on a black horse?"

"Most people have motor cars," Rory said.

"This was a horse—a big black one. It was late evening and I couldn't see distinctly. The rider was a woman."

"Maybe you saw Black Morag," Rory said.

"Black who?"

"Morag. The woman the loch is named for. She used

to live hereabouts and then—well, this was back in the eighth century, of course."

"And you're about to embark on the local ghost story."

"Not that anyone really believes it," Rory said, "but the legend is that Morag rode a black stallion and was very beautiful. Then one day the Vikings raided and she was—" He stopped short, blushed hotly and went on rather hastily, "Well, you know what Vikings did."

"When they'd finished pillaging," Sister Joan said.

"Morag went crazy," Rory said. "She leapt on her horse and rode it into the loch. Since then she's been seen from time to time, galloping her stallion along the shore."

"Have you ever seen her or met anybody who has?"

"No, I can't say I have," he admitted with a sheepish grin, "but some of the old folks roundabout say they knew people who did see her. Me, I think it's just a story. There aren't any spirits."

"None that gallop about on black horses anyway," Sister Joan said. "On the other hand it's possible that certain places can be imprinted vividly with the memory of some tragic event and then under certain conditions—atmospheric, maybe, the event is re-enacted, like a film being reissued. But Morag's spirit, if she ever existed, has been at peace for centuries."

"If you say so, Sister." The mockery had returned to his eyes. "Anyway, that was probably what you saw. You weren't scared, were you?"

"Just curious. Thanks again for bringing the stuff up here."

He raised a hand in farewell and went down the steps at a pace that argued a familiarity with steep places that she envied.

Going back into the cave she emptied the sack, noting that Mrs. McKensie had added several tins of sardines and salmon and a large currant cake. Also, she noted happily, a shiny tin opener. There was something ironic about a woman stocking tinned fish when the local waters must be teeming with fish, but there were still people who didn't think fish was real unless it came out of a tin.

By the time she had put the tins in neat pyramids at the side of the cave, heated and eaten a tin of soup, and washed her bowl, the morning had fled, and her itinerary was shot to bits. The afternoon was supposed to be spent in spiritual reading and exercises, but through the open door the sunlight shafted temptingly.

She closed the door, took her Bible and sat, cross-legged on the floor, her concentration focused on the passage she had marked. If she ever made it through the heavenly gate, she decided, she would love to find out exactly what "Revelations" was all about. The cadences of the sentences had a dreamy quality that half hid, half revealed the meaning. Like spray thrown up from the deep water, half hiding the figure on the black horse— and it had been no ghost. That being so, then why had Rory tried to plant the idea in her mind that it had been? Why not simply tell her who owned a horse and liked riding it as darkness began to cloak the lochside?

"Sister, pay attention," she admonished herself aloud, and heard her voice echo round the cave with a soft, sighing sound that made her wish that she hadn't closed out the sunlight.

THREE

✠ ✠ ✠

Sunday mornings were the loveliest time of the week.
On Sundays one had more leisure to spend in church or
in the enclosed garden of the convent, and the pupils
who came more or less willingly to the little school on
the moor were not around to be disciplined, taught, fret-
ted over. Peace arched its rainbow over the Sunday sky.
It was a time for renewing one's sometimes tenuous
spiritual contacts, for dipping into books there was no
space for in the week, for seeing the little faults and
failings of the other sisters as endearing quirks.

Halfway up the steep cliffs with its iron-railed steps and
the door of the retreat hospitably open, Sister Joan stood
and breathed in the air. The Cornish air was sweet, but
this air was like wine. It made her want to cry out a greeting to the rocks and the pine trees and the loch, shimmer-
ing blue-green far below. She had been awake since dawn,
scrubbing herself thoroughly with cold, soapy water that
made every goosebump stand out, saying her morning
prayers with the energy brought by a sound sleep, and
now, munching an oat cake she stood, watching the light
change and strengthen as the sun rose.

"And that foolish boy lost his faith," she said aloud,
and laughed, hearing her own voice as a sweet ripple on
the air.

Faith, she thought, wasn't something kept in the

34

pocket that could fall through a hole. It was a burning chain about the heart. Sometimes the only way to endure it was to deny it was there at all.

Her mood continued as she swept out the cave and replaced the burnt out candles with tall Sabbath ones she had brought with her. Far below the faint sound of bells danced up to her. The monastery signalled the approach of mass.

She was becoming accustomed to the climb up and down to the cave. Quite apart from the benefit of the exercise she liked the feeling of being high above the world. In the retreat, problems that seemed serious became insignificant.

The shores of the loch weren't deserted this morning. She could see a few soberly clad people pushing out small boats. No more than a dozen including three small children, she calculated. A few Catholics still practising their faith in an environment that merely tolerated them at best. She walked with a springing step, enjoying the breeze on her face.

"Good morning, Sister Joan."

Brother Cuthbert was loping along the shore towards her, the ginger hair about his tonsure fairly crackling with energy. Just to look at him made one feel slightly weary.

"Good morning, Brother Cuthbert." She stopped as he skidded to a halt, seeming to use his large, sandalled feet as brakes in his headlong progress.

"I brought the boat over this morning and decided to offer my services as boatman in case you needed help."

"That's very kind of you. It's years since I was in a rowing-boat," she said gratefully.

"One or two of the parishioners might offer you passage across but as you can see their boats are small," Brother Cuthbert said, guiding her to where a rowing-boat swayed gently at anchor.

"There's only a tiny congregation here too," Sister Joan remarked.

"I understand there used to be many more," Brother Cuthbert said, "but the old ones died out and most of the young ones moved to Glasgow or Edinburgh or even down into England."

"Among the Sassenachs," Sister Joan said gravely, gathering the skirt of her habit and making a neat landing in the boat.

"Sometimes it's necessary if they're to earn a living wage." Stepping in after her he seized both oars and began to flail the water.

"You haven't pulled up the anchor," Sister Joan murmured.

"Sometimes I despair of ever getting my head on straight." Brother Cuthbert struck the offender a sharp blow and hauled up the dripping anchor.

"The old crofters have largely gone now." He resumed the conversation as he pulled away from the shore. "It's my belief the Highland clearances started it all, and there's no use in turning the clock back. Yet it's a good, healthy life. Here's the island now—except that it's only an island at certain times. The tides are queer just beyond the loch. If you were thinking of taking a swim then I'd advise against it—not that nuns generally do, but since Vatican Two the rules have all been changed round, so one can't be sure. I heard of one convent where the sisters are allowed to smoke."

"Not," said Sister Joan firmly, "in the Order of the Daughters of Compassion." They were approaching the reed-fringed shore with its wooden wharf upon which the other members of the congregation were stepping, tying their boats to the sea girdled posts along it. One or two glanced her way and nodded with shy, courteous dignity.

"Watch your shoes, Sister." Brother Cuthbert extended a large hand. "The wood can get quite slippery when the water's high. If you'll excuse me I have to be running ahead of you. If you follow the path you'll come to the church and after the mass I'll row you back again. Or find someone who can handle the boat."

He strode off into a tangle of trees and bushes that grew down to the wharf. There was an unpaved track ahead with stone walls hiding the view at each side, and the bells sounded louder now.

Sister Joan paused to clean her shoes on a tuft of grass and walked on, following the others who looked, she couldn't help thinking, as if they would be more at ease in jeans and sweaters than print dresses and Sunday black.

The church had a low, square tower at one end, and the rounded arches that had preceded the soaring Gothic. The wall dipped down at each side and she saw neat rows of vegetables and beyond a cluster of beehive-shaped huts built of the same grey stone as church and wall. A larger structure with smoke issuing from several chimneys stood a little way off with what looked like a covered passage joining it to the back of the church. As she entered the latter the smell of antiquity was in her nostrils.

The interior was dim until her eyes became accustomed to the candlelight that mellowed the outlines of harsh stone. The altar in the east had a narrow window behind it on which, in stained glass, was depicted a pale, yellow-tinged crucifixion. She wondered how it had escaped the ravages of the Reformation. In accordance with modern practice a simple wooden table stood before it so the priest could celebrate mass facing the congregation. The congregation sat on equally simple wooden benches and a final touch of oldworldliness was provided by the straw scattered on the floor. It linked her with the people who must once have worshipped here—people in rough tunics, knowing only the Gaelic and a little dog-Latin, their ears pricked for any sounds of dragon ships swinging into the loch from the open sea.

Genuflecting, she took her place at the end of a bench and prayed briefly for her sisters in the convent and for the people with whom she would be, albeit briefly, connected during her month at the retreat. The tinkling of the bell brought her to her feet with everybody else as the Father Abbot, as she guessed, entered from the sacristy door, followed by two brothers who were obviously to serve as his acolytes. At the same moment she became aware that benches at the side partly hidden by a wooden grille had filled with cowled figures.

For an instant the scene of which she was a part had the quality of a medieval dream and then, with a little shock, she heard the rich tones of the celebrant intone the Asperges in modern English that jarred upon her for a moment. There were times such as this when she regretted the Latin. Mother Dorothy had occasionally chided her for the opinion.

"It is the meaning behind the words that matters, Sister, not the tongue in which they are uttered. Using the vernacular enables the congregation to participate and brings the mysteries closer to the people."

"Yes, Mother Prioress," Sister Joan had murmured, blue eyes downcast. Perhaps, she had thought and still thought, the words themselves had vibrations that created power to join heaven and earth. It wasn't a view that would be popular so she kept quiet about it, but occasionally she said an Ave in Latin and wished she had been reared in the traditional rituals.

The mass progressed at a brisk but not breakneck pace. The Father Abbot was tall and thin with a halo of silvery hair and a face that reminded her of the paintings she had once seen in Madrid of fine-boned Spanish grandees, with their fingers hovering near the hilts of their swords. It was probably very snobbish of her, she reflected with a glint of humour, but she did like her father abbots to look like abbots and not like anyone you might run into at the local supermarket.

The Kyrie had begun. She had wondered idly if there would be music since there was no sign of any organ loft and then one of the brothers rose and, still standing in shadow, struck the first notes on a lute. Even the first notes sent a ripple down her back. Whoever was playing was a master of the instrument, each phrase exact, delicate, exquisite. It was music to stir the soul, never once descending to banality. Monks and congregation chanted the ancient Gregorian chant as the notes of the lute threaded the words as neatly as pearls on a thin chain of gold.

As the Kyrie ended she risked a glance sideways and caught a glimpse of large sandalled feet and a flash of red hair in the candlelight as Brother Cuthbert sat down again heavily and pulled back his fallen cowl. Now she no longer puzzled over the presence here of that clumsy, good-natured young man.

The sermon was the kind she enjoyed—not too long, not couched in abstract theological terms but nevertheless with depths beneath its simplicity. His voice resonated through the candlelit space.

Somebody was watching her. The first faint prickle of unease ran up the back of her neck. She folded her hands tightly together, forcing her mind into the correct state for the reception of Holy Communion, but the conviction that eyes were fixed unwaveringly and thoughtfully on her back persisted. The stalls where the monks sat were at her left, in such gloom that it was impossible to see if the seats were all occupied, and impossible to pick out individual faces.

"Discipline of the eyes," her novice mistress had impressed upon her, "is one of the most important rules to be learnt. Wandering eyes betoken a wandering mind. Keep custody of your glances especially in church. Make it second nature to yourself."

And that meant, Sister Joan thought, resisting the temptation to raise her eyes briefly from her folded hands on her way back from the altar rail in order to see who stood just within the door and stared at her so intently.

Head bowed and fingers candle-pointed she moved forward with the rest of the small congregation. The monks remained kneeling in their places and the abbot stepped across, moving behind the screen to give them Communion in virtual privacy. Eyes on the straw-strewn floor, Sister Joan returned to her seat and as the feeling of being watched receded gave herself up thankfully to prayer.

The final blessing having been announced she left at the tail of the short procession. Outside the abbot was greeting parishioners, shaking hands, his silver haloed head bent.

Sister Joan moved past on to the track again. The sun was high and hot overhead. It was truly a St. Martin's summer. The three children, released from piety, ran on ahead, scampering like mice between the dipping stone walls.

"Sister Joan?" Brother Cuthbert had emerged and was striding after her.

"The music," she said, pausing for him to draw level, "was truly sublime."

"It's the one thing I can do without messing everything up," Brother Cuthbert said with a cheerful grin.

She liked the calm and modest way in which he accepted his talent and her compliment upon it without any false protestations. There was true humility there, she thought, and recalled with a little prick of guiltiness her own longing to see her work signed and praised on the walls of picture galleries.

"Father Abbot wishes to know if you would be kind enough to take lunch with him," Brother Cuthbert was continuing. "On Sundays he often has guests to lunch in the parlour. One has to keep a certain amount of contact with the outside world even in a monastery."

"Yes, of course. And I'd be pleased to have lunch with Father Abbot," Sister Joan assured him.

"As long as it doesn't interfere with any private vows you might have made, of course?" he said anxiously.

"It's hard enough for me to keep the general rules without thinking up any extra vows," she said, with a chuckle.

"I'll bet you're better at it than I am," Brother Cuthbert said, pushing open a gate and standing aside to let her through. "I seem to be a catalogue of fearful mistakes. We can go this way past the beehives."

"So they're really beehives!" she exclaimed, looking towards the cluster of domed huts.

"Oh no, those are our cells," Brother Cuthbert told her. "The original monks here lived in them before the main building was built behind the church. We still occupy them. The kitchens and the refectory and the infirmary are in the main house and Father Abbot and Father Denis—he's the novice master, though we haven't got any at the moment—they have rooms in the main house too. These are the beehives proper. We get lots of honey from them but it's pretty hard to get it potted and labelled and sold these days—not a viable undertaking."

He was sweeping her onward past bushes whose fragrance made her think of spice jars and Victorian potpourri and butterflies with the sunlight turning their wings to gold.

Behind the church the main building which was attached to the older edifice, as she had guessed, stretched back, its roof low and tiled with chimneys at odd angles. They looked as if they had been stuck on as an afterthought, and when she commented as much to her escort he nodded.

"The fireplaces were put in later on, about the middle of the last century—there was quite a little religious revival going on then. We only have fires in the kitchen and the infirmary, of course. Oh, and in Father Abbot's parlour if he has Sunday guests. Here we are."

He opened a door and ushered her into a long, stone antechamber with nothing in it except a bench.

"Father Abbot will be along in a minute, Sister. I'll go and get my own lunch and row you back afterwards when I'm called."

He indicated the bench and hurried out, almost catching the hem of his habit in the closing door.

Sister Joan sat neatly on the bench, feeling rather like a schoolgirl waiting to be scolded by the head-mistress—or in this case, master. The antechamber was fiercely cold, the chill soaking through her garments and freezing her marrow. She concentrated on controlling her shivering as well as she could. Something else was making her shiver. She looked up sharply and her eyes fastened on a peep-hole high in the opposite wall. A leper's squint? Or a means whereby some long dead abbot had kept close watch on his community. The peep-hole was a lighter square in the darkness of the surrounding stone but she had the impression that someone had just stepped back noiselessly from the small aperture.

An inner door opened and she rose politely as the tall figure of the abbot who had removed his vestments and wore the plain habit of one of the brothers came in, his hand outstretched.

"Sister Joan? Welcome to the community," he said

pleasantly. "I appreciate your accepting my invitation. As Brother Cuthbert will have told you I do have the occasional visitor for Sunday luncheon, but those occasions are becoming few and far between. In the season a handful of tourists stop over at the hotel on the mainland for a day or two and then move on."

"I hope they buy your honey," Sister Joan said.

"It's wonderful honey," he assured her, "but we make such tiny profits on the sales that it's hardly worthwhile. However one likes to keep up the old traditions though it isn't a very efficient way of obtaining an income. This is the parlour. It is rather unusual for a parlour to be built in a monastery, but a century ago the laird's lady, who contributed most generously to the expenses here, insisted on incorporating a parlour so that she could visit without disturbing the rest of the community—not that she was boisterous, you understand, but she was rather good-looking, so they say, and might have provided too much of a distraction."

The room into which they had stepped was of moderate size, the original stone of the walls covered with panelling, the floor covered with a decidedly shabby red carpet but with a bright fire crackling in the fireplace and with variously hued cushions cheering up the dark furniture.

"Only a simple repast, but one must avoid gluttony," the abbot said, with a humorous little sigh. "One of my greatest trials in the religious life has been my love of good food beautifully cooked. My father, God rest his soul, was by way of being a master chef and I was brought up on nouvelle cuisine before the word had even been invented. Fortunately Brother James has a fine hand with the fish fryer—fresh trout, Sister, and new potatoes and salad, and in honour of my guest a glass of white wine. It is some considerable time since we had anyone in the retreat."

"Brother Cuthbert was very kind to me when I arrived," Sister Joan said, taking the chair he had pulled back from the gate-legged table.

"An excellent young man," the abbot said. "I wish more like him were attracted to the monastic life, but that seems to be the main problem in most communities these days."

"We have the same problem in our order."

"The world is too much with us, I suspect. Let me help you to the fish, Sister. I had the heads removed."

"I'm glad," she said frankly. "I hate to see my lunch looking back at me." The abbot shot her an amused glance and passed her the butter sauce. Monks, she reflected, still kept the old hospitable customs that made their cuisine far more varied and exciting than the dishes served up in her own convent. The wine he poured was an Alsatian, not too sweet. The glass was thin and delicate with a faint tracery of lead at its base.

"To more vocations." He raised his own glass in a ceremonial little gesture.

He was a man, she thought, raising her glass in reply, who still craved the small luxuries of politeness. She wondered if he had been brought up in an hotel, had watched the guests coming and going, seen them off guard as they chatted and commented on the dish his father had just sent up from the kitchens. It was none of her business, however, she reminded herself sternly and setting down the glass, said brightly, "I was most interested in your church, Father Abbot. It must be very old."

"Seventh century—or to be more exact the original church stood on that site. It was of wood, but the Vikings had a nasty habit of invading at regular intervals and in the early ninth century the present stone structure was built and consecrated. Very little has been altered since then. We don't even have a telephone line here."

"But surely in cases of sudden sickness?"

"Which so far seldom happens, thank God. Should there be such an alarming incident it takes only five minutes to row to the mainland or even to use the stepping stones at certain times. And we have Brother Stephen who is a splendid infirmarian with several first-aid certificates. So we really don't worry."

"How nice to hear someone say that," she said softly. "There's so much strain in the world today."

"I suspect there always was," the abbot said, looking amused again. "It cannot have been very pleasant to have to live here knowing that at any time the carved prows of the dragon ships might round the cliffs into the loch. And of course I was referring only to health matters. There are other worries to beset us—a lack of vocations, shortage of funds—upon my word, if we allowed our novices to smoke hashish and have pop concerts we might get more takers."

"Gigs," said Sister Joan.

"I beg your pardon, Sister?" He gave her a puzzled look.

"Pop concerts are known as gigs these days," she explained.

"Are they really? How very interesting," he commented. "Not that I am thinking of holding one. A—gig. In my grandfather's time that referred to a wheeled cart on which dashing young gentlemen escorted their lady friends. More salad?"

Sister Joan shook her head. "It's delicious, but I don't have a huge appetite," she said.

"We're largely self-supporting here," the abbot told her. "The climate can be harsh but the air is remarkably pure as we don't have to contend with the noxious fumes emitted by cars and lorries, and fortunately one or two of our brothers have green fingers and could make roses grow on a rock. Now we will have a russet apple which is my favourite of all the apples and a cup of coffee. Are you managing in the retreat?"

"I'm getting used to it," Sister Joan said cautiously, biting into a tart russet, "but I didn't really expect to be comfortable. Hermits are supposed to rough it, I think."

"I take it you are not a natural hermit, Sister," he said, paring skin from the fruit he had selected with a small, silver knife. "Fortunately it is now being recognized that nearly everybody requires some form of human contact. Of course there are the exceptions who may be honoured but seldom imitated. Your own convent is in Cornwall, is it not?"

"High on the moors," Sister Joan said. "We too are largely self-supporting. I've only been there for a year. I went from the mother house in London."

"Where Mother Agnes is the prioress at present?"

"Yes, she is. Do you know her?" Sister Joan felt a surprise that she always felt when two people living far apart proved to be known to each other.

"Many years ago," the abbot said. There was a slight twinkle in his eyes that made her long to ask under what circumstances they had known each other, but she ate her russet and sipped the rather weak coffee demurely.

"You have sufficient in the way of literature with which to sharpen your mind while you are here?" he was continuing.

"Very little, but I hope to do some painting while I am here," she said. "It has always been a great interest of mine and my present mother Prioress, Mother Dorothy, suggested that I might spend some of the time painting local scenes. I keep reminding myself that I'm

here to renew my spiritual life and not to enjoy myself
doing what I like."

Reaching the end of the sentence she blushed as she
realized that she could have phrased it more neatly, but
the abbot merely nodded.

"The two are not incompatible," he said. "Was it not
St. John of the Cross who, being discovered playing
with a duckling, said he was worshipping God? Have
you thought of sketching the church here? It's very ancient as I said and in certain lights quite breathtakingly
atmospheric."

"Would you mind my doing that?" Her face lit up. "I
wouldn't want to disturb the community but it would be
marvellous to try to capture it with the enclosure
stretching around it."

"Come over when you choose," he said kindly. "Ar-
range it with Brother Cuthbert. He can row you over in
the boat on the mornings you wish to paint."

"That's very kind of you."

Privately she decided that her first task would be to
make a sketch of the church as a small return to the abbot for his kindness.

He was beginning to rise, a flattering degree of disap-
pointment on his strongly-marked features.

"The brothers will have finished their luncheon by
now," he said, "which means that duty calls me again.
Except on the rare occasions when there are visitors I
take all my meals with them. If you wish to have another look round the inside of the church please do so.
Brother Cuthbert will row you back to the mainland
when you're ready."

"Thank you for a wonderful luncheon, Father Abbot." Shaking hands with him she surprised another
flash of humour in his eyes.

"Don't go starving yourself while you're here, Sister

Joan," he said. "I know that even girls in convents these days cannot resist this foolish slimming craze."

He really was rather an old duck, she decided, as she withdrew. Not many people referred to her as a girl these days though she wasn't yet thirty-seven. She suspected that in his youth he must have been quite a charmer.

He had held the door open politely for her and she crossed the antechamber to the outside without remembering the peep-hole. The good food had restored her usually commonsense attitude. Now she was apt to think that she had imagined that someone was watching her in the church, spying on her as she waited for the abbot. The trouble with being a nun was that one grew accustomed to living in a community with someone constantly at hand in times of trouble. Probably a little loneliness would do her a great deal of good.

She followed the lines of the covered passage to the front of the church again and went in. The candles were still burning and the sweet, sharp perfume from the copper censor hung on the air. She walked slowly to the altar and stood looking up at the crucifixion window behind, its delicate yellow tones like dying sunlight in the gloom. So many generations had worshipped here; so many prayers were folded into the crevices of stone. It would be almost impossible to paint the interior unless one was a Rembrandt, but she reckoned she could do justice to the exterior.

A faint shuffling sound caused her to turn her head sharply in time to see the sacristy door at the left of the altar softly closing. This was certainly no flight of the imagination. The idea of someone spying on her while she contemplated the sacred symbols struck her as peculiarly unpleasant. Before she had given herself time to think she had stepped over the altar rail and pulled open the side door.

A room with wall cupboards which held, she knew, the various vestments required for the feasts and services of the church met her gaze. There was a tiny modern window fitted at a slight angle into the wall, and a further door at her right. Sister Joan stepped across and opened it, frowning as her eyes fell on stone steps curving down steeply. There was an electric light bulb burning which surprised her for a moment until she saw the battery fixed on the wall.

Second thoughts might have caused her to hesitate. Sister Joan, who nearly always acted on her first thoughts, went swiftly down the steps with her hand sliding down the curving iron rail fixed as banister.

The steps curved round into a tunnel with a rough, concave roof and a floor formed from packed earth and stones melded by the centuries into a rough surface. By contrast the walls looked smooth, the blocks of stone gleaming faintly in the light from a second light bulb set high and jutting out at an angle.

"Is someone there?" She raised her voice as she strode forward and her words echoed back to her in a series of diminishing "here—here—here." The air was dry and cold and the tiny stones under her feet crunched as she moved forward.

Within a few yards the tunnel curved to the left. She reached the corner, turned it and was plunged suddenly into darkness.

Some kind of time switch had evidently been rigged up. She paused abruptly, trying to work out where the nearest switch would be. Presumably there was one to enable the light to be switched on from both ends of the tunnel. She took a cautious step sideways and felt along the wall. Her fingers trailed smooth stone and then met empty space. She stumbled slightly to regain her balance and her outstretched hand touched flesh with the unyielding hardness of bone beneath. For an instant fright locked her tongue. Then she snatched her hand away and backed down the tunnel again, feeling along the wall where she had just walked while her voice released itself into a jumble of words.

"Stop playing stupid games. Who are you? Why are you watching me?" Her words were cut off abruptly as she banged into the wall. The tunnel had become narrower or perhaps she had backed the wrong way. She stood still, her heart thumping, hearing suddenly a new sound. Footsteps were echoing through the darkness, echoing all round it; the soft padding bounced from wall to wall.

Dim light glowed again as someone pressed a switch. She opened her mouth to call again and was transfixed in a new kind of horror. Inches away from her a leathery brown face grinned sightlessly into her own.

"Jolly looking chap, isn't he?" said Brother Cuthbert, walking into view. "He died in the eleventh century, I think. Father Abbot says the dry air has helped preserve them all, almost as if they'd been embalmed."

"All?" Her voice emerged as a slight croak as she hastily moved further out of the shallow niche into which she had stumbled.

There were other niches, each one occupied by a seated, black-robed figure, dry darkened skin stretched over dead bones, rusty habits hanging about them.

"All former abbots according to the records," Brother Cuthbert said. "They had new habits a hundred years ago. I think they were supposed to be kept here as an honour, but the custom died out ages ago. In the 1500s. Rather touching to think of them all grouped here together while above them the life of the monastery goes on."

"Very touching," Sister Joan said dryly. Her breath was still coming in little gasps. "Shall we go?"

"I can turn on the light again if it goes out," Brother Cuthbert said helpfully. "However—since we're not really supposed to be here because the air can alter the temperature we'd better leave, I suppose."

The horrid boy sounded positively regretful, she thought indignantly, as she walked rapidly ahead of him to where the curving steps began.

"The cloister walk is just above us," said Brother Cuthbert, following. "That's the bit that joins the main house to the back of the church and—"

"How did you find me?" she interrupted.

"Father Abbot told me to come over to the church to meet you. When I got here the sacristy door was open—"

"How did you get here?" she interposed.

"Along the cloister walk." Brother Cuthbert closed the door to the crypt and gave her a slightly bewildered look. "There's a door at the right of the altar in the old choir stalls where the community sits. Why?"

"I just wondered," she said feebly, remembering to genuflect as they came into the church again and turned briefly to acknowledge the altar. "I thought I heard someone in the sacristy."

"Brother Jacob is the sacristan but he's been in the refectory all the time since mass," Brother Cuthbert said. "Mind you, he's getting on a bit, so it's likely he left the door ajar before mass and nobody bothered to close it. Is it important?"

"No," said Sister Joan, wondering if she was speaking the truth. "No, of course not. I'm sorry I kept you waiting. Are you ready to row me across?"

"Any time you're ready, Sister." He sounded gallant. "Father Abbot says you are going to do some painting of the outside of the church. It's really the community's chapel but it's been years since there was a Catholic church over on the mainland, so now it serves both functions. On what mornings were you thinking of coming?"

"Tomorrow and after that it depends on the weather and how fast I'm getting on, but if I could get hold of a small boat I could row myself across."

"It's no trouble," he said quickly. "Honestly, Sister, I'm not much use in the community except for fetching and carrying and doing a bit of luting, so it makes a nice change to have a regular task."

"A bit of luting." She shot him an amused glance as they walked down to the shore. "Yes, one could describe it as that. Where did you learn to play so well?"

"Royal College of Music." He looked suddenly shy. "I got a scholarship. The tutors thought I ought to take it up professionally, but I never wanted to play in public. I mean, can you really see me as a member of an orchestra? It's daft. Coming to Loch Morag was the best thing I ever did. I came on a hiking trip and stayed on. It's a grand life."

They had reached the boat and she stepped down into it cautiously from the slippery wooden wharf.

"I hope those old abbots didn't give you a shock." He took up the oars. "I don't mind them myself, but they are a mite creepy, I suppose. And you were actually touching one, you know."

"Don't remind me," she said. "The light went out and I was feeling along the wall for a switch and—"

"They can't hurt you, Sister." He spoke reassuringly as if he were years older than she was. "The dead must be the most harmless creatures on earth."

"Yes. I know." She spoke sombrely, her eyes on the rippling waters as the oars parted them. The dead were indeed harmless, but the hand she had grasped in the darkness of the crypt had been warm, full-fleshed—and alive.

FOUR

✠ ✠ ✠

Mondays were pale blue days, Sister Joan thought, when she woke up the next morning. As a small child she had seen time as great swathes of colour—orange for Tuesdays, honey-brown for Wednesdays, green for Thursdays—and Monday had been the palest of blues, clouds stretched across the sky like crisp linen on a washing-line. In that respect Scotland wasn't disappointing her. When she stepped outside the retreat the pristine freshness of the air went to her head like wine and she found herself singing her first Ave aloud, a song that broke into laughter when a small, inquisitive bird swooped down from above, peered into her face, and took off again, adding its own cry to the melody.

"It's good to be alive!" she exclaimed.

The fears of the previous day had receded and assumed more sensible proportions. Monks were human, she had reasoned, and the presence of a female, albeit a nun, had roused one to curiosity. Perhaps the one who had watched her disapproved of women on the island and had found a way of frightening her off. At that thought she set her jaw in what her family had come to recognize as "Joan's obstinate look," and resumed her devotions more circumspectly. It was rather a nasty trick for a religious to play, her thoughts ran on, but on the other hand her own besetting sin was that of impul-

53

siveness. She had had no business to go poking around in the crypt.

Having settled the mystery to her own satisfaction she completed her chores, gathered together her painting materials and made her way cautiously down the stone steps and the scree below to the shore of the loch. There were several boats on it this morning, the boatmen crouched over their fishing lines. Away on the horizon the sun had risen, gilding the dark rocks and making the surface of the water glisten with a million dancing motes.

"Good morning, Brother Cuthbert!" She hailed him cheerfully as she spotted him further along, pulling his boat into shallower water, apparently in blissful disregard of the fact that his legs were soaked almost to the knees and the skirt of his habit clung to his shins like a wet dishrag.

"It's a day for rejoicing indeed," he returned. "Sometimes I think God sends us these days in autumn so that we can remember them when the winter comes. Father Abbot says you may paint what you wish inside or outside the church and you may leave your things in the scriptorium. You won't want to lug everything over and back again every time you come."

"That's very kind of him." She jumped into the boat and sat down, surprising a look of admiring astonishment on Brother Cuthbert's face.

"My word, Sister, you're spry for . . ." His voice trailed away.

"For my age?" She grinned at him. "Strictly between ourselves, Brother Cuthbert, I'm in my mid-thirties, so I do wish you'd stop treating me as if I were a senile old lady."

"Sorry, Sister." He grinned back companionably.

"Granted," she told him, and chuckled for no reason

but that it was a fine morning and he reminded her of one of her own brothers.

When they reached the wharf he carried the painting easel and folding-stool and tucked the case where she stored paints and canvas and palette under his arm, holding them above water level but getting his habit more disreputable as he scrambled through the shallows. Tying up the boat, having made a somewhat neater landing, Sister Joan looked round her with the anticipation of pleasure.

In this clear light the grass was rainbowed and the grey stones of the little church had a warm patina that made her fingers ache to capture it in paint.

"The scriptorium is at the back of the main house," Brother Cuthbert informed her when they had reached the church. "It's sort of stuck on next to the kitchens. Just go in when you feel like it. There won't be anyone there at this time of day and, of course, you can leave your stuff there when you're ready for me to row you back."

"I'm causing you a lot of work," Sister Joan said. She spoke somewhat absently, her fingertips itching to start.

"Glad of it," Brother Cuthbert said. "I'll be back later then."

She nodded, her gaze riveted on the church with the pre-Gothic arches, the low, square tower at the end. She would make several sketches, she decided, and then work two of them up into paintings—the church in summer daylight with the wild herbs springing about its foot and the church as she imagined it would be on an evening with candleglow gilding the windows and scattering gold over the snow.

Jacob had teased her that her work was stuck in the romantic period, that only cameras were for literal representation. His own work was brilliant, spiky, often difficult to interpret. She wondered if it had mellowed in the years since they had gone their separate ways. Had he reverted completely, found a pretty Jewess who could give him Jewish children? She hoped so. Jacob had been a man who needed another person to complete him.

An hour later she had half a dozen rough sketches on her pad. She smoothed out the shadows with her fingers, realizing that she was thirsty. Perhaps there was a tap or spring around where she could drink. At any rate she'd take a look at the scriptorium since she needed to leave her heavy equipment there. The next day she would begin to translate her sketches on to the canvas, starting with the summer background.

She packed away her pad and pencils and lugged easel and stool in the direction Brother Cuthbert had indicated. Over the low wall she could see some of the monks busy among the vegetables. Bent over hoes and spades they never lifted their heads.

The main building was fortress-like with its uncompromisingly square design. Only an occasional slit of window broke the solid surface of stone. She guessed there was probably a central yard with a well in it and the inner windows looking out on it. Despite modern concessions the monastery was still a very private place. Her nose led her to the back where a couple of doors stood wide with the unmistakable smells of cabbage and onions wafting through them.

A youngish monk—she guessed a lay brother—came to the open door. His sleeves were rolled above muscular forearms and he was holding a large pan.

"The scriptorium?" she ventured.

The lay brother nodded towards the left where a stone building jutted out.

"Thank you, Brother."

Walking away she was conscious of a not altogether approving scrutiny at her back. Evidently the abbot was more go-ahead in his attitude than some of his community.

The scriptorium was deserted, the shelves that lined one wall crammed with books, a podium in one corner holding a huge, illuminated manuscript with a fine brass chain locking it down. Presumably a tradition from the olden days, since she figured it was highly unlikely for anyone to try stealing the heavy tome with its steel-bound leather covers. There were a few high-backed, hard chairs and some filled, unlit oil lamps, and against another wall a long table on which bottles of coloured inks and pens were ranged alongside large sheets of paper on which someone or other had been practising the ancient art of lettering.

A further door in the corner led, to her relief, into a small lavatory, with a washbasin. When she turned the tap water trickled out, reluctant but clear. She scooped some into her hand and quenched her thirst.

Footsteps sounded in the long apartment beyond. Sister Joan hastily pulled the door closer, feeling a sudden shyness. Emerging from a lavatory was nothing to be embarrassed about, she reasoned, but on the other hand she had no desire to disrupt the quiet monastic routine by any sudden appearances.

The footsteps paused uncertainly. She had a sense of someone looking round, and then, through the crack left between door and wall, issued a long sigh—no, more of a groan, she thought uneasily.

It wasn't repeated and, after a moment, she heard the footsteps retreating again. Somewhere a door closed.

She waited a moment more and then came out into the scriptorium again, looking about as she did so.

Nothing had been disturbed. She frowned, hearing again in her mind that long-drawn-out heavy sigh. The footsteps had been heavy. Someone wearing boots? The monks she had seen wore sandals but she supposed that for some tasks they wore sturdier footwear. But what had brought one of them in here? Had she been watched and followed again?

"Sister, you're getting neurotic," she muttered aloud, frowning impatiently at the illuminated manuscript on its stand.

Something had been changed. The open page of the manuscript had displayed square cut characters in a mixture of red, gold, and blue. She had noticed the initial letter B with a butterfly skittering about it. The initial letter now was a D, and instead of a butterfly there was the head of a horse drawn in black ink dappled with gold. She went closer, bending over the manuscript. Perhaps it was the custom to turn a page every day. Carefully she turned back the heavily decorated vellum. No, the letter A was five pages before this one. She smoothed the page down again and wrinkled up her nose in puzzlement.

"Sister, we're not supposed to touch that."

The monk who had directed her here stood in the doorway, his face and tone highly disapproving. He had exchanged the pan he'd been carrying for a tray which he now set down carefully on the end of the long table. There were some biscuits, a couple of apples, and a jug of water and glass on it.

"Someone just did," Sister Joan said. "While I was in the lavatory I heard someone come in. They—whoever it was—turned forward five pages."

"Only Father Abbot touches the Morag manuscript, and he never turns five pages at once," the monk said. "I brought you some lunch, Sister."

"Thank you. The Morag manuscript, you said?"

"It's what it's known as but it's a Book of Hours that some sixteenth-century laird had made for him by the brothers here. It has the story of Black Morag in it, with prayers for her soul."

"Does this page tell that story?" She indicated the manuscript and the other came over to look, still holding himself at a little distance as if he feared she might suddenly leap forward and bite him.

"My Latin isn't very good," he said, "but I think that's the page, yes. The title letter has the horse's head."

"The horse on which she rode into the loch after the Vikings went away."

"She lost her mind, poor soul," the monk said quickly, as if Sister Joan had uttered some personal criticism. "I must get back to my duties. Leave the jug and glass here and I'll collect it later."

Not to save her trouble, Sister Joan reflected as he went out again, but to keep dangerous females out of his kitchen. The notion that she might be regarded as a dangerous temptation made her want to giggle.

Crossing herself, murmuring a grace, she set to on the biscuits and the apples, demolishing the lot and drinking a couple of glasses of the cold water. There was certainly a well somewhere on the island. The monks were almost entirely self-supporting. She wondered how large the community was—no more than twenty, surely, and probably fewer since the abbot had mentioned the lack of novices.

And had it been the abbot who had crept in to turn the illuminated pages and then sigh deeply? It seemed unlikely. Perhaps her too vivid imagination was playing tricks but she was sure that the person who had turned over the pages was the same person who had watched her during mass and spied on her through the peep-hole in the antechamber.

The problem had no solution because she wasn't even certain if there was a real problem at all. If anyone particularly wished to speak to her there didn't seem to be anything in the rule to forbid it. These were not Trappists, vowed to silence. She shrugged her shoulders impatiently, and went out again, leaving her painting equipment but carrying her sketch book and case of pencils.

As she walked towards the church one of the figures leaning over a spade beyond the enclosure wall stuck it into the earth and came striding after her.

"Would you be wanting to go back now, Sister?" Brother Cuthbert wiped his hot face with the sleeve of his habit and smeared soil across his brow.

"If it isn't a trouble?"

"Not a bit of trouble," he assured her. "To tell you the truth, Brother John will be delighted to be rid of me. I'm always rooting up what ought to stay in the ground and leaving weeds to flourish. You found the scriptorium?"

"And left most of my things there. I've finished some preliminary sketches, and tomorrow I want to start translating them on to canvas. When is it possible to walk across on the stepping stones?"

"Only when there's a freak tide and that only happens a couple of times a month these days," he informed her. "They're not really stones either, but the sheared off tops of fossilized tree trunks. Thousands of years ago the loch was much narrower and there was a long strip of land with trees on it that joined our land to the shore, but the sea ate it away and the trees fossilized. The water there used to be very low indeed and someone had the idea of shearing off the trunks and reinforcing them with iron to provide some kind of causeway, but the tides changed and now the water's hardly ever low."

"So it wouldn't be safe for me to try it?"

"Not a bit safe, Sister," he said firmly. "Anyway I enjoy rowing. Watch your step now."

"The pot," said Sister Joan, nimbly boarding the small vessel, "ought not to call the kettle black."

"I've yet to do penance for getting my habit soaked," he said ruefully, glancing down at his sea-rusted garments. "As Father Abbot is always telling me it's a sin against holy poverty to be careless about one's clothes. The trouble is that it's not easy to find a penance that isn't pure pleasure for me to do. I mean, can you imagine doing anything more satisfying than praying?"

Sister Joan, who had always considered it would be more of a penance to be forbidden to pray, concurred with enthusiasm and they gained the shore in high good humour.

"See you tomorrow morning. God bless, Sister." He pulled away strongly as she alighted, judging her distance nicely and landing on a solid tussock of grassgrown earth with reeds pointing the way to heaven all around. The loch was almost deserted now, the fishermen having presumably gone home for a meal, and only the diminishing shape of Brother Cuthbert in his boat peopled the solitude. Sister Joan moved higher up the dry ground and sat down with her back against the cliff. This was a wonderful place to meditate in, with the sky arching overhead and the loch spreading its ruffled waters like pleated silk before her. Had it been thus, she mused, in Galilee when the fishermen had sat, sharing bread, each busy with his own thoughts, all waiting for the young man with the intense gaze who widened horizons every time He came by?

Stones and pebbles spattered up painfully into her
face, and she let out a yelp as she opened her eyes. Between her and the sunlit water a dark shape loomed, and
she shaded her eyes with her hand, preparing to launch
on a blistering reproof.

"I didn't see you there," said a voice indignantly.
"Why, you scared Rob Roy half to death!"

"I was praying and never heard you coming," Sister
Joan said defensively.

"Churches are for praying." The girl with long dark
hair dismounted and stared down accusingly. "Not out
here."

"Anywhere's for praying," Sister Joan said trying to
sound mild, but irritably conscious that the other was
trying to put her in the wrong.

"Well, you're a Catholic so you'd be bound to have
peculiar ideas anyway," the other said scornfully.

"Sister Joan."

Scrambling to her feet she held out her hand and,
finding it ignored, leaned to pat the horse instead.

"Rob Roy doesn't like strangers," the girl said.

"I take it he's a Protestant horse," Sister Joan said,
having achieved mildness, outwardly at least.

"He's my horse," the girl said.

"And you are . . .?" Sister Joan gave her a questioning look.

"Black Morag, of course!"

"Of course," Sister Joan said promptly. "You've
worn very well over the centuries."

A reluctant grin struggled to life on the pretty mouth
and was killed by a scowl.

"I'm Morag Sinclair," the girl said. "My father is the
minister here."

"I hope he's more tolerant than you are," Sister Joan
said.

"You're not likely to meet." Morag had turned and was mounting up again. She was in her early twenties, Sister Joan reckoned, and certainly lovely but she would have been lovelier had her expression held more tranquillity, and had her voice been gentler.

"And has better manners," Sister Joan added.

In reply Morag jerked her head and set off at a trot that sent another shower of pebbles leaping up. The breeze, catching her hair, tugged it into a dark tail that streamed behind her.

"Well, well, well." Sister Joan gazed after her thoughtfully.

If Morag Sinclair was an example of the attitude of most of the local people then it was no wonder that Dolly McKensie and her son kept themselves to themselves. No doubt Dolly had blotted her copybook by wedding a Catholic in the first place. Sister Joan felt a little wave of sadness at the intolerance that sprang up in quite small places and marred the unity of the human race.

Her peace of mind had been disturbed by the intrusion and she walked back slowly to where the slanting scree led to the steps of the retreat. The girl had been, she was prepared to swear, the same dark rider who had galloped along the shore on the evening of her arrival, the girl about whom she had asked Rory. And Rory, instead of saying, "She's Morag Sinclair, daughter of the local minister," had launched out into a romantic legend and a possible ghost. All of which told Sister Joan, whose female intuition was quivering like the whiskers of a cat stalking a bird, that there was some connection between Rory McKensie and the rude young woman on the splendid horse. Sister Joan, who had always enjoyed a bit of genuine romance albeit vicariously, wondered if an association between them was forbidden by their families and at the same moment imagined only too clearly Mother Dorothy's probable comment.

"Capulets and Montagues, no doubt! Two teenage tearaways if you ask me." Except that her prioress was unlikely to use the word "tearaway" which would have smacked too much of modern, slipshod slang.

It was as she began to walk up the slope between the clustering pines that she heard herself hailed from behind.

"Sister Joan? Good afternoon."

"Good afternoon, Mrs. McKensie."

Sister Joan paused and turned to enable the older woman to catch her up.

Dolly McKensie, out of her shop, looked curiously rootless, the sunshine inexorably deepening the lines on what had been a pretty face, the grey in her hair more pronounced. She had taken off her flowered overall but her print dress and cardigan looked limp and depressed.

"I'm not interrupting you?" she asked, catching up.

"I'm glad to have the opportunity of thanking you for the extra groceries," Sister Joan said cordially. "I was hoping you'd allow me to pay you for them."

"It was a gift." Dolly spoke almost sullenly.

"Then I thank you for it," Sister Joan repeated.

"Been over to the monastery?" Dolly glanced out towards the island. "I've never been there myself. Seems a funny way to live, shutting yourself away from everybody like that—begging your pardon."

"It takes a particular kind of vocation. Like marriage." She stopped abruptly, feeling like kicking herself for her tactlessness.

"Which my husband never had," Dolly said, the dark residue of an old bitterness in her voice. "Funny when you look back to see how clear everything is, isn't it? Alasdair married a non-Catholic from out of the district.

I used to think that he'd chosen me because he loved me too much to let rules and regulations matter, but the truth is that he married me because he intended to carry on with his bachelor pleasures afterwards and he'd not insult a girl of his own faith by doing that. Not that he was any great shakes as a Catholic for all that. Never went to mass from one year's end to the next. It was me who saw to it that our Rory got to go to First Communion and all the rest of it. His dad took no interest in any of it, but I've a couple of aunts over in Aberdeen—not Catholics themselves but High Church. They got the local Catholic priest to see to Rory's First Communion and his Confirmation later on. We went over to stay with them while it was all being done. Alasdair never came near."

"I'm sorry. It was very good of you to take such trouble," Sister Joan said gently.

"Not that it did any good in the end," Dolly McKensie said. "After his dad went off Rory took right against religion of any kind and I never did much to try to argue him out of it. Anyway that's a long time ago. Are you enjoying your stay here?"

"My period of retreat—yes, very much. I teach in a small school most of the year, so it's wonderful to get a breathing space."

"Oh, you do work then?" Dolly sounded unflatteringly surprised.

"Yes indeed," Sister Joan said. "Ours is not a completely enclosed order. Those sisters who are constrained to earn a living outside the convent have leave to do so. Our earnings go into the general kitty. At the moment I'm the only one with an outside job, but one of the other sisters grows and sells vegetables and some of the others make illuminated cards and calendars. So we aren't as idle as many people suppose."

"So a retreat makes a bit of a holiday for you," Dolly said. "Well, there's many a time I've thought of doing the same thing myself—just shutting up shop and heading for the Costa Brava or somewhere."

Sister Joan, privately disagreeing as to the similarity between the Costa Brava and a cave high up a Scottish cliff, murmured something indeterminate.

"Mind you, when things get a bit much I can always put the Closed sign up for an hour and come for a walk," Dolly said.

"Doesn't Rory mind the shop while you take a break?"

"Rory has his own life to lead," Dolly said shortly. "You haven't seen him this afternoon, by any chance? Sometimes he—he does a bit of fishing."

So she had followed her son, Sister Joan thought. And she doubted if Dolly had been interested in checking on his fishing. She was sure of it by the red that dyed the other woman's sallow cheeks when she said, "I'm afraid that I haven't. I met another local person though—Morag Sinclair? She said she was the minister's daughter."

"So I believe. I've never met her personally." Dolly McKensie spoke with a different air—constrained and sharp. Her hands were clenched at her side and her mouth had thinned.

"She was riding her horse along the shore," Sister Joan said. "Rather an abrupt young woman, I thought."

"Sly," said Dolly McKensie. "Or so I've heard tell. Her father's a widower and cannot do a thing with her. Behaves as if she owns the loch. Not that I know her personally."

"Does Rory?" Sister Joan asked the question impulsively before she could remind herself that it was none of her business.

"Rory has more sense!" his mother said angrily. "Anyway she's three years older than he is—and as stuck up a fine piece as you'd find anywhere north of the border. Well, if you'll excuse my chatter, you'll be wanting to get on, Sister."

Without any further farewell she turned and scrambled awkwardly down to the level ground again, taking off at a rapid pace without looking back.

Definitely a case of the Capulets and the Montagues, Sister Joan decided, watching her go. It would be interesting to meet Morag's father and find out his views.

She turned and went on up the steep hill, framing her mind to prayer again. The lives of those she met were not her business.

Not her business but they intruded on her spiritual disciplines. For the rest of the afternoon she struggled unavailingly to lose herself in contemplation. It was useless. No sooner had she fixed her mind upon a particular aspect of the Divine when questions jostled for supremacy in her mind. What jealous instinct had led Dolly McKensie to walk along the shore in search of her son, and why did she clearly believe that Morag Sinclair wasn't a suitable friend for him? The age difference didn't seem to be so very wide. And why did Morag herself behave like a spoiled brat and an intolerant one at that? Sister Joan remembered. Had she learnt her bigotry from her father? And why should anyone in the monastic island follow Sister Joan herself and try to frighten her?

Impatiently she rose from her knees and went outside, leaning against the outer side of the cave and letting her gaze rove over the loch. The sun in sinking had dyed the loch crimson and already a faint Jacob's ladder traced its silvery path across the water. She couldn't see the village from this side of the cliff but on the opposite shore of the loch a light sprang up. There was, she saw for the first time, a large house there, its dark stone blending into rock and pine. From this vantage point it was the only sign of habitation, since it was necessary to walk a little way along the shore before one glimpsed the island with the narrow spur joining it to the opposite shore and the hidden causeway of fossilized tree trunks hidden under the water between the near shore and the wooden wharf.

On impulse she descended the steps, feeling the chill of the approaching night and telling herself firmly that a brisk walk would chase away the cobwebs and put her in a more receptive mood. Mother Dorothy was a great advocate of exercise in moderation to balance the activity of the mind. Sister Joan wondered if it would work in her case. Unless she could find answers that satisfied her the spiritual benefits of the retreat would be lost for her.

She reached level ground and crunched her way along the shingle. When she reached the spot where her meditations had been interrupted earlier she sat down, her back against the rock. Overhead a nightjar cried a warning, and she caught the glint of the first moonray on its wings. Beauty was all around her if one had eyes to see. Humour too, she mused, as a plumy-tailed squirrel landed only a few feet away from her and sat up on its haunches to nibble at a supper snack of hazelnuts. Soon the creature would be seeking the warm womb of the earth as protection against the cold. God must have enjoyed creating squirrels.

A sound caused the squirrel to bound nervously away. Not from Sister Joan herself for she had sat as quiet as stone, but a slithering noise from further along the beautiful, night-purpled shore.

Cautiously she turned her head and saw that someone

was pulling a boat out of the shallows on to the shore. She must have lost herself more fully than she realized in thoughts of creation since she had heard no splash of oars as the boat approached the shore.

Her first thought had been that it must be some fisherman out late in pursuit of his supper, but the figure bent over the prow was cowled and hooded, too far off to be identified. Some instinct held her motionless as from the pines further along the cliffs another figure stepped quickly and with a nervous glance over her shoulder. Then both figures walked side by side into the pines together and the moon rayed on an empty boat.

She discovered she was shivering violently. Rising and treading with caution on what patches of rough grass she could find between the stones she put a safe distance between herself and the others—Morag Sinclair with her long hair unmistakable and her tall companion, concealed in the habit of his order.

When she gained the section beneath the retreat she went up scree and steps as rapidly as if it were still full light, feeling as if, in some way, by her very presence she shared in whatever sin might be.

FIVE

✠ ✠ ✠

She had slept badly, her dreams full of dark, running figures who alternately chased her and were chased along a never-ending shore. When she finally slept without waking the dawn was streaking the walls of the cave with narrow, tentative fingers. She woke with a little yelp of dismay, her senses telling her it was almost nine o'clock even before she squinted at her fob watch.

"No breakfast for you, lazybones," she castigated herself, stumbling to the back of the cave to splash her sleep-blurred eyes with cold water.

By the time she had finished her prayers and tidied the disordered blankets, mute evidence of her restless night, the pale dawn had become mellow gold.

She climbed down the steps and gained the shore, feeling the warmth of the day like a benediction. She would begin the first of the paintings she had planned today—an exterior of the church in summer. It would be presented to the abbot, she resolved, as a small return for the kind hospitality she had been shown.

Brother Cuthbert was already waiting, whistling cheerfully as he chose flat stones and skimmed them across the water.

"Good morning!" Sister Joan greeted him cheerfully as she approached.

"Good morning, Sister." He ceased whistling and

gave her a somewhat embarrassed grin. "Sorry about the noise. Father Abbot would be shocked at such levity."

"I used to whistle myself," Sister Joan admitted, accepting a guiding hand into the boat. "Not since I entered the religious life though—save in moments of great stress."

"I whistle because I enjoy it," Brother Cuthbert said simply, looking as if stress was a foreign word to him.

"Yes," Sister Joan said with equal simplicity. Enjoyment, she had always thought, should be accounted as one of the virtues.

"Excuse my mentioning it, Sister, but you look tired this morning." He shot her a glance from under reddish brows.

"I didn't sleep well. I thought that—I suppose some people go night fishing on the loch?"

"I suppose so. I never thought about it," he said with a faint air of surprise. "We go to bed at nine in the monastery so I've never really seen. Why?"

"No particular reason," Sister Joan said vaguely. "It must be lovely to go for a moonlight sail, don't you think?"

"Not when one is doing the rowing," he said, with another grin. "No, I look forward to my bedtime, Sister."

Then it hadn't been Brother Cuthbert who had pulled his boat up to the shore and vanished into the woods. On the other hand he would hardly admit it if it had been him. The nasty little suspicion wound its way into her thinking.

"Watch your step, Sister."

They had reached the wharf and she jerked herself back into the moment, but some echo of her troubled thinking must have reached her companion. As they walked up the track between the high walls he said hesitantly, "Sister, I've been thinking about Sunday. I mean your being in the crypt."

"Where I had no business to be."

"You said something about someone else being there?"

"When I was in the church," Sister Joan told him, "I was convinced that somebody was watching me through the sacristy door—it was partly ajar. It was an unpleasant sensation and I went into the sacristy to find out if—and blundered into the crypt."

"You know, Sister." Brother Cuthbert's face had reddened almost as brightly as his hair. "Do forgive me for saying this, but sometimes—when a lady reaches a certain period of life—she starts thinking that maybe she's being followed. My mum had a neighbour who went quite—quite . . ."

"Dotty?" Sister Joan suggested, and found herself laughing helplessly.

"It was most irregular of me to have mentioned it," Brother Cuthbert said unhappily.

"How young you are!" She wiped tears of laughter from her eyes. "Oh, forgive me for laughing. It was at myself as much as at you. Perhaps I am going peculiar, but I promise you it has nothing to do with my time of life. No, I am certain that someone was watching me when I was in the church. I had had the same feeling earlier during mass, and when I was in the anteroom waiting for the abbot I thought that someone looked down from the peep-hole in the wall."

"Sister, you can't mean that!" He was as white now as he had been red before. "That someone from the community should spy on you—I can't believe it."

"Perhaps I was mistaken," Sister Joan said kindly. It was a shame to spoil the clear crystal of his boyishness.

"Some of the older brothers," he confided, "were actually a bit uneasy when they were told that you'd be coming over to do some sketching and painting. They felt that having the lay community here for mass on Sundays was quite sufficient. Brother Alphonsus saw you as the thin end of the wedge, I'm afraid."

"I'll try not to get in the way," she promised gravely.

"And I've my duties to do. I'll see you later, Sister."

He turned and strode away, clearly still a trifle embarrassed at the direction the conversation had taken. No, it couldn't have been Brother Cuthbert who had gone into the pine trees with Morag Sinclair.

She walked on round to the scriptorium. The door was open and nothing seemed to have been disturbed since the previous day. She walked over to the podium, noting that the illuminated manuscript had been turned forward by one page. Moving to the long table against the wall she collected her things, hitching the easel under her arm and carrying the folding-stool somewhat awkwardly in the other hand.

The church had a mellow kindliness about it this morning. It looked, she thought, like a place that had grown up of itself out of the surroundings. Along the base of the walls tiny wild flowers sang their last song of summer.

Within a few minutes she was immersed in the task of transferring the sketch she had made into a faint outline on canvas. Then there were the oils to be mixed and that first heart-thrilling moment when she touched the bristles of her colour laden brush to the outlines traced on the canvas. She took a deep breath and a tiny flower in the lefthand corner sprang into life.

The morning flew by on wings. When she finally raised her head at the sound of footsteps the sun was directly overhead.

"There's a bite ready for you," said the newcomer. It was the disapproving monk who had brought in water and biscuits the previous day. This morning he looked, if anything, ever more frowning.

"That's very kind of you, Brother . . .?" She hesitated.

"Brendan," he said curtly.

"Brendan the Voyager," Sister Joan said impulsively. "It is most kind of you, but I really don't expect to be fed every day."

"It's little enough," she was surprised to hear him say. "I'll carry the easel if you like. If you've finished painting, that is."

"For today." She added hastily, "It's still wet," as he bent to pick it up.

"I'll take care. Give me the stool. Right then."

Having apparently exhausted his conversational range for the time being he strode ahead without waiting for her. Sister Joan picked up what was left and followed him meekly to the scriptorium where he deposited his burdens, jerked his head towards the tray and went out again.

Today there were oat cakes thinly smeared with honey, a large pear, and a mug of distressingly weak tea. After a fasting morning everything tasted delicious.

When she had finished she damped down a cloth and hung it carefully over the half-completed painting, checked that her belongings were stowed neatly to one side and went out into the sunshine again. The door to the kitchen was pointedly closed and she made a small grimace as she passed. Brother Brendan evidently considered her a dangerous temptation.

She walked back slowly to the church and stood for a few minutes looking at its ancient façade. To go inside and spend a few precious moments in worship was too good an opportunity to miss, and she pushed open the door, dipping her fingers into the holy water stoup, blessing herself and moving on into the dim light that filtered through the leaded windows. Apart from the sanctuary lamp only a couple of candles burned on the altar. She slipped to her knees, feeling the straw prickle them, feeling that in this place straw was more fitting than deep-pile carpet.

The sacristy door was open again. She came slowly out of her prayer to feel a slight draught on the side of her face, to hear the faint click as the door closed again. An unreligious indignation bubbled up in her. This really was intolerable. To be followed, watched, and spied on was ruining this period of contemplation and spiritual renewal on which she was embarked. She was on her feet again in a moment, passing within the altar rail, opening the door, her voice calling ahead of her into the empty room, "Who is it? Who's there?"

The door leading to the crypt softly closed. She stared at it for too long a moment, then, with a suppressed exclamation of annoyance at her own nervousness, stepped across and wrenched the door open again.

Echoing back to her were the slow footsteps she had heard before though the stone steps were deserted. The light bulb burned dimly and the air was still. Her desire to follow warred with the cold chill of unease that rippled through her. It was foolish and she despised herself for it but for several moments superstitious fear held her in a vice. The light went out and she looked down into a dark void only faintly lightened by the daylight in the room where she stood.

She could close the door, go back into the church and wait for Brother Cuthbert to come and fetch her for the short journey to the opposite shore. Then she would spend the rest of the day blaming herself for cowardice.

She pressed down the light switch on the wall and without allowing herself to create any more monsters went swiftly down the steps into the tunnel. Some part of her had registered the position of the light switches and she walked rapidly, turning the corner where the tunnel widened and became the crypt proper. She had steeled herself for the alcoves with the seated figures and this second view of them was less horrific than her imaginings. The flesh had long since dwindled from their bones and the tight stretched skin was brown and leatherlike. Yet it was still possible to see traces of the men they had been in the arch of eyesockets and the curve of a proud, medieval nose. She located the second light switch and pressed it down hard, hoping to capture the light for a few more minutes.

A half-burned candle standing on a narrow ledge attracted her attention. It had been wedged into a tin holder and the box of matches on its rim placed it as belonging firmly in the twentieth century. She lit the candle hastily and felt calmer. That primitive part of herself which feared the dark was stilled and she found herself breathing more easily. Even when the bulb went out she wouldn't be floundering about in obscurity.

The bodies, she now saw, were seated on stone and iron with straps holding them in position. They were no more than shells after all. Men who had once been abbots ruling the community above through periods that were now history. She walked more slowly, looking for an exit. She had felt no draught blowing the other way but the man she had followed must have left by some means or other.

The light went out and the flame of the candle she was holding streamed up high. She gave herself no time to fear the shifting shadows but raised the candle higher and pressed the switch again. It was at that moment she saw the door—a slab of oak weathered to the consistency of stone at the corner of the far wall. It had neither bolt nor keyhole but when she inserted her fingers into the depression at the side she was able to pull it open without too much effort. A further flight of stone steps wound upwards, leading to the covered passage that connected the church to the main building, she reckoned. So whoever came and went, watching her movements, would now be among the other members of the community. She pushed the door shut again and looked round at the silent, seated figures.

Shells. Mere shells with life, vitality, personality, and soul long since fled. She made a mental note to pray for them later though she doubted if they were still in need of prayer, and found herself observing them with more compassion and less timidity. It was even possible to hazard a guess as to their ages. One or two had the contours of youth. It was a pity their names had not been scratched into the stone, but probably they had sought a modest anonymity.

As the light went out again her hand suddenly shook, sending her shadow trembling across the wall. What she had just noticed, she told herself, groping for the switch again, must be a figment of her imagination. She groped for the switch again and took a closer look, her breath coming raggedly.

No, she hadn't imagined anything. The figure who sat motionless in cowl and habit at her left hand had the tip of a leather shoe poking out from the hem of the skirt. The other bodies wore sandals or the remains of sandals. She bent down, lifting the garment higher and saw that both feet were encased in extremely dirty but undeniably modern shoes with laced fronts and what looked like matted woollen socks underneath.

She didn't know what significance her discovery had, but at that moment her overriding instinct was to get away as quickly as possible and think about her discovery. Turning, she went rapidly back the way she had come, set the candle on its ledge, and prudently pressed the light switch again before she blew out the flame. Then she made her way up the stairs and into the sacristy again so fast that she had to pause to catch her breath. When Brother Cuthbert stuck his head in at the church door she was advancing to meet him.

"Are you ready, Sister? I'd not want to interrupt your prayers," he began anxiously.

"I wasn't praying," Sister Joan said truthfully. "I was thinking."

"Oh?" He gave her a politely questioning glance as they came out into the open.

"About the crypt. Has—would you know when the last abbot was placed there?"

"A couple of hundred years ago, I think. Father Abbot has the records of names and suchlike. Nowadays everybody gets buried in the usual way in the enclosure cemetery at the other side of the island—well, isthmus actually since we're joined on to the opposite shore."

"I noticed a large house there," she said.

"The Sinclair house. The Sinclairs used to be lairds here, but after the Highland Clearances the old clans dispersed. The minister lives there now—the Protestant one, but he's a connection of the old family."

"And has a daughter called Morag." She shot him a quick glance but his face remained free of embarrassment or guilt.

"I believe so, though I've never spoken to her," he said.

They had reached the boat. Climbing into it, Sister Joan ventured a further question.

"I suppose the bodies in the crypt are never moved?"

"Why would they be?" He gave her a puzzled look as they pulled away from the wharf. "The air has preserved them, and since hardly anyone goes into the crypt they're left in peace."

"But someone rigged up a light there."

"That was Brother Matthew—before my time. He liked to pray in the crypt, but he was old and his legs were getting a bit shaky so Father Abbot gave him leave to rig up a light. Why, Sister?"

"Idle curiosity," she said vaguely.

The body she had seen had certainly been there for less than two centuries. She hadn't looked much at the face which, as far as she recalled, was already showing the dried, leathery look, but the shoes, despite their filthy state, had been modern, and she had a shrewd idea that under the habit there would be modern garments too.

"Will you be coming over tomorrow, Sister?" Brother Cuthbert asked.

She hesitated, biting her lip. She would have to take another look at the body before she decided what to do. Her first impulse to find her way to the nearest police station was fading. Local public opinion didn't favour the community, and the arrival of the police would not only cause talk which might be damaging but also disrupt the tranquil routine of the monks. She would have to take another look before she made up her mind what to do.

"Sister?" Brother Cuthbert was waiting for her answer.

"If it isn't any trouble to you, Brother," she answered

quickly. "I made a good start on the painting and I'd like to finish it if possible."

"The weather might be breaking soon," Brother Cuthbert nodded, "and you'll not want to be sitting outside in the rain."

"True." She smiled her thanks as she alighted. "Tomorrow then. I do so appreciate your kindness."

"It's good exercise." He raised his hand in farewell and began rowing strongly away again.

She had landed in the shallows and her shoes and stockings were wet. Sister Joan had no particular fear of getting cold but she did fear slipping on the steep cliff that had to be traversed before she reached the retreat.

Reminding herself that Daughters of Compassion met every eventuality with a smile—a rule she honoured more in the breach than in the observance—she made herself as comfortable as possible on an outcropping of rock and took her shoes off. The sun blazed down in most unseasonal style and she wriggled her toes hoping the stockings would dry fairly soon. Her shoes were caked with shale and salt water; she pulled up a handful of grass and set to work to clean them. At her back the clustering pines dropped their dark needles as the wind rose and entered into competition with the sun.

This was the way the cowled boatman had come and Morag Sinclair had met him. She stood up and turned round, her shoes in her hand, and frowned at the narrow path that wound between the smooth trunks. It would do no harm to take a short stroll.

Pushing her damp feet into her shoes and lacing them up she walked into the green shade, the waters of the loch glittering behind her.

The path twisted and turned in a manner that made her feel slightly disorientated and came at last into a sloping patch of bare rock above which the cliff loomed. The ground was thick with pine needles and on the lowest slope a beech tree flamed orange and scarlet.

Something white caught her eye as she looked round. She stared at the beech tree for a moment, then went over and stood on tiptoe to reach the paper caught in its branches. It was only part of a sheet of paper that had obviously been torn by the wind. Sister Joan turned it over and read the few sentences penned at the top.

". . . and feel your sweet mouth against mine and the little fluttering breaths of desire that move me more than the most passionate poetry of love. If we could declare our feelings then the world in which I live would be more beautiful than even the Creator intend—"

"Yuk!" said Sister Joan.

The bottom of the page had been ripped in irregular fashion. By the wind as she had first thought or had the recipient scorned the effusion? If so, that showed her good taste—or his? No, the handwriting was square, black, and very powerful. She knew her opinion would probably be regarded as sexist but she was almost sure it was a masculine hand. And either wind or hand had torn it, flung it into the tree.

She folded it and slipped it into the deep pocket of her habit, and circled the tree looking for more glimpses of white, but there were none.

The memory of the cowled boatman and of Morag Sinclair walking softly along the twisting path came too vividly into her mind. None of this was her business, since she wasn't either her brother's or her sister's keeper, but she felt a deep disquiet as she emerged on to the shoreline again and began to walk along the shale.

82   Veronica Black

The crunching of footsteps towards her caused her to raise her head, her mind still on the puzzles and problems that had loomed up. They were swept away, for the moment, at least, as she beheld the tall figure approaching. Against the light she had an impression of solid blackness which resolved itself into long dark overcoat and shovel hat. Between the two a face, sallow-skinned, square-chinned, and dominated by black eyes, was set on wide shoulders.

"You," said the newcomer brusquely, "will be the Romanist nun."

"I'm Sister Joan," she agreed, "and you will be—the minister?" It had been a bow drawn at a venture but he nodded, still retaining his hat, and said in the richly rolling voice that she could easily imagine thundering from a pulpit, "Alexander Sinclair, yes."

"How do you do?" She started to put out her hand but as he showed no sign of having noticed it withdrew it again.

"I was by way of seeking you out," Sinclair said.

Her heart sank a little. Alexander Sinclair looked like one of the stern Covenanters who had ruled by fear over their flocks and the prospect of being warned off by him was a daunting one.

"Are you allowed to eat?" he demanded abruptly.

"Now and then," Sister Joan said, taken off guard by the enquiry.

The minister frowned even more forbiddingly, his square jaw jutting. Then he said abruptly, "I live at the manse across the loch. Dinner this evening? I'll send a boat. You eat meat?"

"Only on Christmas Day and at Easter," she informed him.

"We'll have salmon," he said. "Be ready at seven."

"I—yes, thank you." She stared after him as he

turned and walked away, heading evidently for a small boat moored further up the shore.

An invitation to the manse from a man who from everything she had deduced disliked Catholics and wanted them out of the district struck her as odd. Or was he hoping to pump her for information about the monastic community? The thought was an unpleasant one. She thrust it aside and went up the needle-clad slope towards the retreat.

Not until she had been wrestling in prayer for over an hour did it occur to her to wonder if the invitation would in some way help her to resolve her present dilemma. God usually worked in mysterious ways.

"Too mysterious sometimes," she said aloud, and rose from her knees to make herself a cup of tea.

SIX

✠ ✠ ✠

Before 6:30 she was waiting on the shore, her long coat wrapped around her to protect her from the wind that had risen and was tugging spitefully at her veil. Just past the narrow gully that provided a short cut to the railway track and the village meandering over the next hill were the remains of an old jetty. Guessing that the boat would pick her up there she made her way to the spot, watching the occasional light glint out as the dusk folded itself around the loch. Soon the weather would change and the cold come. She wondered if fires were allowed in the monastery. Probably not. In her own convent the infirmary where the oldest members of the community lived out the remaining days of their lives was always pleasantly warm, as was the big kitchen where the lay sister did most of the cooking, but everywhere else was chilly after winter set in.

The boat was coming. She raised an arm and felt a slight tremor of unease as Morag stood up, pushing back her long dark hair and called ungraciously, "You'll have to get your feet wet. I can't come in closer."

"Won't," Sister Joan muttered, stooping to remove shoes and stockings. With them in her hand and her skirts hitched knee high she waded into the shallows and clambered aboard, aware of mocking dark eyes. Morag was certainly attractive and would have been lovely if her mouth had turned upward at its corners and her eyes had held some spark of humour.

"Thanks ever so much." Sister Joan sat down and gave the younger woman a broad smile.

"For what?" Morag asked, sounding surprised as she lowered herself to the oars again.

"For giving me the opportunity for a spot of penance," Sister Joan said blandly. "Modern monastic living is so soft that one never gets the chance to catch pneumonia."

"There's a towel on the seat," Morag said after a moment's pause.

Sister Joan fished it out and rubbed her feet and legs before shooting a look at the figure opposite. "Will I be paddling ashore at the other side?" she enquired.

"There's a wharf there and steps," Morag said, not turning her head. Sister Joan resumed her stockings and shoes with some thankfulness.

The waters of the loch were choppy as the wind strengthened. The trip across was more than twice the distance that Brother Cuthbert rowed her when she visited the island. To walk right around the loch would take hours, she reckoned, and decided that she might undertake it before she went home.

"It was kind of your father to invite me," she said aloud.

"Highland hospitality." There was a slight sneer in the other's voice. "If outlanders come to stay he feels it incumbent on himself to invite them."

"And now you have given me another marvellous chance to feel humble," Sister Joan said. "I might have been in danger of fancying myself specially favoured otherwise."

"You're bloody sarcastic for a nun," Morag commented.

"Meekness," Sister Joan said, "is not one of the virtues I feel most comfortable about."

Unexpectedly she heard a smothered chuckle from the other end of the boat which was turned hastily into a coughing fit.

"Maybe I shouldn't have said bloody!" Morag sounded suddenly uncertain.

"I've heard worse."

"Not in the convent!"

"No, not there." Sister Joan hesitated, then said, aware that she was dangerously close to contravening the rule that one's previous life sank into anonymous insignificance when one entered the religious life. "I was an art student once. Some of the language used in so-called Bohemian circles would make your toes curl up. What career are you following?"

"I don't need a career." The sulkiness had returned to Morag's tone.

"Nor want?"

"Not particularly. I'm thinking of breeding horses."

"Sounds like a good idea." Sister Joan spoke mildly, relieved that the further shore was looming. People like Morag Sinclair brought out the worst in her.

There was a jetty in good repair and she climbed out of the rocking boat with alacrity and waited for Morag to tie up the craft and join her. The other girl was wearing breeches and high-necked sweater and would have graced any magazine cover.

"This way." Morag was already striding ahead, snapping on a large torch as she negotiated a broad steep driveway interrupted at its most sheer by short flights of steps cut out of the rock. Above them lights glowed in the house—a two-storey granite house with two rows of small windows set one above the other and what looked like a series of terraces along its façade. Behind the house the tall, thin triangles of pine showed black against the upper reaches of the cliff.

"It looks like a fine house," Sister Joan said.

"It takes a lot of upkeep. Parts of it are sixteenth century." There was the unmistakable hint of pride in Morag's voice.

"But it's your home."

"Yes. Yes, it is."

She had quickened her pace, leaping up the steps that joined one terrace to the next and leaving Sister Joan to follow as best she might. It was fortunate, the latter thought, that light from the windows above provided some illumination else she might well have slipped and fallen.

As they reached the top terrace the deeply recessed front door opened and a woman with an apron on that glittered white against her dark dress appeared in the aperture, calling, "Come away in, Morag! I'm to serve if you're any later."

"Jeannie housekeeps for us," Morag said, going before Sister Joan into an arched hall that was lit by an inadequate light bulb and fell into darkness again beyond a narrow flight of stairs. The floor of polished stone was uncarpeted and the cold struck to the bone.

"You'd best get yon breeches off and a decent skirt on," the elderly woman said scoldingly. "If you'll wait in there?"

She indicated an open door on the left and without any further greeting went grumblingly towards the back of the hall while Morag ran up the stairs, her heels striking smartly on the stone.

The room on the left was a parlour, a fire in the grate still pale and newly lit, a dresser towering against one wall dominating the meagre space. Two uncomfortable-looking upright chairs flanked a round table on which a number of silver framed photographs of Morag at various ages from babyhood on were arranged. The room had a fussy, Victorian feel. Sister Joan sat down on the edge of one of the chairs and hoped the fire would blaze up soon.

"Sister—Joan? Good evening to you. My daughter got you here safely then?"

Alexander Sinclair had come through a door at the other side of the room. In dark clerical dress with a narrow white dog collar he seemed too big for the room.

Hoping that Morag hadn't been expected to tip her overboard, Sister Joan rose, extending her hand and then clamping it to her skirt again before he could refuse to shake hands.

"Yes. It was a most comfortable trip," she said, not mentioning the wet start.

"She rows well. Morag does most things well." The man's voice had imperceptibly softened. "Come into the dining-room. I can offer you a sherry or a whisky?"

"A very small whisky and water, please."

"A good choice. Whisky is more warming." He had turned back to retrace his steps with the lack of formal good manners that seemed defiant in Morag but in him gave the impression of forgetfulness rather than deliberate rudeness.

The dining-room was a larger room with a carpet that didn't fit it entirely and left a wide margin of unpolished wooden boards around its perimeter, and curtains of a vivid and incongruous medley drawn across the windows. The long table was laid for three at one end with what looked like delicate china and heavily-chased silver cutlery, and there were several high-backed chairs with their seats covered with rubbed and faded velvet.

"Sit down, Sister. I've no doubt that Jeannie'll be sounding the gong as soon as Morag changes out of her heathenish trousers," Sinclair said, pouring whisky and adding water liberally to the glass. "Sip your drink now. You'll likely be unused to strong drink. I wish I could say the same about some of my parishioners. I will join you in a drink though I seldom indulge."

It was, she supposed, the standard excuse of the drinking man but the minister with his air of good health and sturdy frame was probably speaking the truth, she reckoned. Seen in the somewhat brighter light cast by the rather elegant chandelier he was younger than she had first taken him to be, mid-forties with close cropped black hair peppered with white and a face lined more by intensity of feeling than by age.

"It seems a pity to dilute a good whisky," she said, "but you are right—apart from wine on festive occasions spirits are not generally drunk in the convent. Your health, Mr. Alexander."

"Minister will do—unless you object to the term?" He shot her a quick glance as he seated himself at the head of the table.

"Of course not."

"You make a virtue of tolerance, I see. Someone said once that tolerance is only another name for indifference."

"Somerset Maugham and he was only half right. It depends on what is being tolerated."

"You are probably right. Your health, Sister. How are you enduring that medieval cave where your superiors have deposited you?"

"I daresay it's the modern equivalent of being walled up alive," Morag said, sweeping into the room and catching the tail end of her father's comment.

She had changed to good effect, Sister Joan thought, the rich garnet shade of the long caftan she wore a per-

fect foil to her black hair, now drawn back and fastened
with tortoiseshell combs.

"Did you know that despite all the legends there is no
documentary proof of any nun ever being walled up
alive?" Sister Joan said.

"Surely where there's smoke there's always a little
bit of fire?" Morag said, seating herself at the other side
of her father and glancing at him with the kind of shy
longing for approval that a much younger girl might
have shown.

"I think that some of the stories might have arisen
during the medieval period," Sister Joan said. "Becoming a hermit became quite popular at that time. Many
lay women received permission from their parish priests
to immure themselves and rely on the charity of the
neighbours for a regular supply of food."

"Sounds like a good way of avoiding a brutal husband," Morag commented as Jeannie came in, put a tu-
reen of soup on the table, and withdrew.

"There were not many ways in which women could
express themselves in those days," Sister Joan agreed,
as the younger girl rose and began to ladle out the soup.
"Anyway in those far off times there were often out-
breaks of plague and famine—sometimes whole communities could die off."

"And the hermit would be mistaken much later on for
someone who had been deliberately starved to death?
It's an ingenious theory." Sinclair gave her a faintly
mocking look.

"It's a possibility," Morag said with a grudging air.
"There's bread in the basket, Sister."

The soup was thick with herbs and vegetables. The
bread was coarse and dark with flakes of wheat in it.
Sister Joan was surprised when Sinclair said, "Your
cooking is excellent as usual, Morag."

"You made this?" Sister Joan flushed slightly at the tactless astonishment in her own voice. "I'm sorry but I assumed that Jeannie—"

"Jeannie cleans and sweeps and makes rice puddings, but she likes her soups out of tins and her bread ready sliced in a plastic bag," Sinclair said, with a faint gleam of humour. "Morag, on the other hand, loves cooking. When she weds, her husband will be a fortunate man."

"I don't intend marrying," Morag said coldly. "I've told you before, Father, that I don't want to get married."

"Morag told me that she was thinking of breeding horses," Sister Joan said, in an attempt to lighten a sudden heavy silence.

"That may bring in some money," her father said. "This manse needs a lot of heating and some extensive repairs doing to the roof. My congregation dwindles year by year as the younger people move away to look for work. Soon I shall be forced to write my memoirs or something."

"You must have had a very interesting life," Sister Joan said.

"But not for public consumption," Morag said sharply, reaching for the empty soup bowls. "There's the salmon with new potatoes and a salad. I haven't had time yet to whip up anything fancy."

Nor, said her eyes, the inclination to please an unwanted guest. The salmon, when it came, was firm fleshed and delicate with a thin aspic glaze and a garnish of lemon slices and cucumber butterflies. Once again there were murmurs of appreciation as they helped themselves from the dishes that Jeannie brought in. There was no wine, she noticed, and was glad of the plain water. Luxury made her uncomfortable.

The meal progressed with occasional comments from

the host—mainly short, inoffensive anecdotes of his youth when he had been a theological student in Glasgow, an amusing story about some tourists who had spent a fortnight looking for the monster until it dawned on them they were in the wrong loch. He spoke well and fluently and Sister Joan felt quite at her ease by the time coffee and fruit were served.

Morag, she noticed, seldom joined in, but ate in almost unbroken silence, her eyes on her plate. Her earlier unfriendliness was palpable, but it seemed clear that it didn't derive from her father's opinions.

"Another cup of coffee, Sister?" He indicated the pot with its heavily-chased design of thistles and roses.

"Thank you, no. If I take a second cup I'm liable not to sleep a wink," she said.

"I wonder you manage to sleep at all," Sinclair remarked, "stuck in a cave halfway up a cliff."

"It really is very well fitted up," she hastened to say. "Any previous hermit would consider I lived in the lap of luxury, and, of course, it's only for a month. After that it's back to work."

"You work?" He sounded surprised and faintly disbelieving.

"We're only semi-enclosed," she explained. "We earn what we can within the limits of the rule to keep the convent financially viable. I teach in a small school on the moors—mainly gypsies and farming children who aren't old enough for the main school or simply refuse to go. So that's my regular job."

"Your secular job," Sinclair said. "Your main job is praying, I suppose."

"Yes. Yes, it is." A little surprised at his understanding she smiled.

"It has always been my custom," he said, with the

glint of humour she had noticed before, "to size up the opposition."

"We don't need them here," Morag said in a low, tense voice, stabbing a pear with her fruit knife. "Catholics are all liars and hypocrites."

"Morag, that is patently untrue and very rude to our guest." Her father spoke sharply.

"I'm afraid that Morag isn't alone in her opinion," Sister Joan said lightly. "There are some very worthy sisters I have met who would use a very long spoon were they required to sup with someone of a different faith. And in the village when I went shopping the welcome wasn't exactly overwhelming."

"Prejudice dies hard," Sinclair agreed.

"And we don't need that clutch of monks on the island," Morag muttered. Sister Joan bit hastily into an apple to prevent herself from enquiring if Morag were trying to break up the community by the simple expedient of seducing one of its members.

"They do no harm," her father said. "There have always been monks on that piece of land. The land itself used to provide a refuge in the days when the Vikings came raiding. And the cave was once a look-out point."

"Yes, so I understand. I'm painting a couple of exteriors of the church and so Brother Cuthbert, one of the community, rows me across and keeps me up to date with ecclesiastical history."

"I've never been across to the place," Sinclair said. "The abbot invited me for dinner once, but my congregation practically threatened to leave in a body were I so unwise as to accept. So I declined with thanks, but one day I may seek to renew the offer of acquaintanceship."

"What are your parishioners going to say about my coming here?" Sister Joan asked.

"It is close on fifteen years since the abbot issued his invitation," Sinclair said. "We had not long resettled in the area and I was more dependent on the approval of my congregation then. Nowadays I would use my own judgement."

"It's getting late," Morag said hintingly. "I've some letters to write so if I'm to row you back . . .?"

"I'll row Sister Joan back myself," her father said. "If you want to go and write letters then we will both excuse you. Morag has many friends from her school-days and sends them such long letters that I am at a loss to understand what on earth she can find to say. Since she acquired a typewriter her correspondence has become enormous."

"I like to keep in touch," Morag said, scowling. "Ex-cuse me, Sister." She swept out of the room with the of-fended air of Lady Macbeth who has just been informed that Banquo's ghost has turned up.

"My daughter was educated at a boarding-school," Sinclair said when the door had closed. "She should have gone on to university eventually, but my wife died six years ago and Morag elected to come home and take her mother's place. She is not an easy person to know but once known she has a very attractive personality."

Not wanting to argue with a fond father Sister Joan held her peace.

"She used to be quite friendly with young Rory McKensie," Sinclair was continuing, "but I believe they don't see as much of each other as formerly."

"You don't object?" Sister Joan couldn't help asking.

"Because he is her junior? That doesn't signify, and though he's nominally a Catholic he hasn't practised his faith in my recollection. However Morag tells me that she has no interest in him."

But Morag was obviously seeing somebody, Sister

Joan mused, and Rory McKensie's mother clearly suspected it was her son. And disapproved of it, she recalled. The tides of prejudice ran in odd channels here with the minister who might have been expected to disapprove being unexpectedly tolerant and yet his daughter betraying her dislike of anything to do with Catholics openly. If that was true then what was she doing, meeting a cowled figure coming from the island late in the evening? Perhaps her apparent intolerance was a cloak to cover a relationship that would be disapproved of by everybody.

"You look tired, Sister."

Her host's voice broke into her thoughts and made her jump.

"I am used to plain food and early hours in the convent," she apologized.

"And find company tiresome?"

"No, my problem is that I like company very much indeed, and that often interferes with my contemplative life," she said ruefully. "I was very glad to be offered this opportunity to get right away and refresh myself spiritually—but please don't think that I haven't enjoyed myself. The meal and the company have both been delightful."

"And now I will row you back across the loch," he said cordially. "There is a promise of rain in the air so we had better get you ashore again before it begins. I have enjoyed this evening, Sister. I suppose it will be of no use to hope that it may be repeated?"

"I'm afraid not but it isn't because I wouldn't want to come," she said regretfully.

"Then thank you again for coming."

They had both risen and he put out his hand, shaking hers firmly for the first time. An intensely reserved rather than a prejudiced man, she thought, and stood waiting as, saying something about fetching her coat, he left the room.

There was a fire burning here too but the corners of the room were chilly. Evidently the minister's stipend didn't provide central-heating.

She moved over to the high mantelshelf and looked up at the portrait of Morag hanging over it. It was a vivid rendering of Morag's dark loveliness but in the portrait at least there was no trace of the sulkiness she displayed in real life.

"My late wife," said Sinclair, coming in with the coat.

"Your wife!" Sister Joan hastily rearranged her ideas. "They are very much alike."

"In appearance but Catherine was of a very gentle, timid disposition. She was very much younger than I was when we married—only sixteen and a very immature sixteen whereas I was a somewhat elderly twenty-three. But we were happy together. Very happy."

"She died young then?" Sister Joan put on her coat and fastened it.

"Only thirty-four," Sinclair said. "Morag was seventeen. She was in her last year at boarding-school when it happened. A tragic accident."

"Oh?"

"Catherine suffered from insomnia," he said heavily. "She tried to cut back on the sleeping tablets her doctor had prescribed; like myself she felt the habit was addictive, but she needed them if she were to get any sleep at all. She tried very hard and naturally I encouraged her in her efforts, but after several weeks without touching the tablets she took her regular dose. Unfortunately she took some double-strength tablets that had been prescribed for an emergency and they were too strong for her. She died."

"I'm very sorry," Sister Joan said. "How tragic that something intended to alleviate her complaint should have—it must have been a very great shock."

"Six years takes the edge off one's grief," he said. "Morag was very deeply affected but I am hopeful that one day the right young man will come along, and she will stop feeling that it's her duty to bury herself here."

Sister Joan murmured something vague. Morag Sinclair had impressed her as a self-willed young woman who only stayed in the manse because it suited her. Then she reminded herself that she had, at first meeting, taken Sinclair to be a harsh, intolerant man. Clearly her first impressions were not very accurate.

There was no sign of Morag or of Jeannie as they crossed the icy hall. Sinclair paused to take down a heavy jacket from a hook. He had, she noticed, already changed his shoes for knee high boots.

Outside the wind blew more strongly and she felt a decided qualm at the prospect of being rowed across the loch in a small boat, but Sinclair, snapping on a torch to illumine the stepped terraces, said cheerfully, "It may get a bit rough later on. Watch your step, Sister."

She watched the step and reached the jetty where the boat bounced threateningly at its moorings. To her right she could see a mass of tangled barbed wire and fallen masonry.

"The spur of land that joins this side of the loch to the island," Sinclair said, noting the direction of her glance.

"Hardly a right of way," she observed dryly.

"No indeed. During the Second World War there was a look-out tower erected to keep an eye out for submarines. After the war the buildings were demolished, but since technically speaking the land belongs to the community it was their right to leave the way blocked which the abbot at that time insisted on doing. It's been left like that."

"It further isolates the community, I suppose," she said, settling down in the boat.

"Surely you would approve of that?" He cast off the mooring ropes and took up the oars.

"In any enclosed order," Sister Joan said, "the keys are on the insides of the doors. A barrier that prevents either access or egress doesn't meet with my approval. It must be quite an eyesore in the daylight."

"Fortunately most of it is overgrown with weeds and brambles," he said, "and the numbers of tourists have dropped off in recent years. People prefer to go to Spain or down to the south coast where they can be sure of warm weather. You had better hold on tightly, Sister. The water is a mite choppy."

Exaggeration was not apparently among the minister's failings. Sister Joan hung on to the seat grimly as a wave splashed up into her face.

"You don't," she spluttered, "have any monsters in this loch, I hope?"

"Not as far as I know." His short bark of laughter was muffled by the wind.

She gasped as another shower of icy droplets blew into her face. Getting uncomfortably wet seemed to be a penance thrust upon her rather than one she had chosen for herself.

They were approaching the wharf and she heaved a sigh of relief, as he jumped ashore and waded through the boiling shallows, dragging the boat after him.

"Give me your hand, Sister. There you are!"

She was on wet and shifting shale but at least she hadn't been expected to wade to land as he had done.

"Get yourself something hot to drink as soon as you

reach the cave," he ordered in his brusque manner. "I'll bid you good evening, Sister."

He was already turning to push the boat into the heaving water again. Sister Joan contented herself with calling a goodnight and turned to hurry along the shore to where she must climb the slope and gain the steps leading to the retreat. It was unfortunate that she had forgotten to bring her own torch. Once or twice she stumbled and regained her balance with some difficulty.

The wind was stronger now and it was beginning to rain. The pines were deep rooted but their needles made the ground treacherous and once, as she struggled up the slope, she found herself on hands and knees.

"A very suitable position for a Daughter of Compassion," she said aloud, and pulled herself upright again, bending towards the slant of the land and grimacing as the wind tugged her backwards. With intense relief she seized the iron handrail and began to mount the steps, trying not to think of the increasing distance between herself and the pebbled lochside.

She had left the door on the latch and with a feeling of homecoming she stumbled within. It was cold here but at least the wind and the sea spray were banished. Her bed with its coarse blankets looked inviting, and once she had lit her candle the shadows retreated to the back of the cave.

She brewed some tea and drank it milkless and scalding until her chilled frame was warm again and she could pay due attention to her evening devotion. She made it longer than usual, adding thanks for the pleasant meal she had enjoyed, remembering to pray for the soul of Catherine Sinclair and for the well-being of her widower and daughter. There had been no opening in the conversation to enable her to introduce any questions about the crypt. In any case the minister had never visited the community.

Not until she was in bed, the blankets wound round her and a second cup of tea warming her insides did she find herself thinking about the events of six years before. In that quiet district the normal tenor of life had been interrupted twice—by the disappearance of Dolly McKensie's husband and the death from an overdose—accidental?—of Sinclair's wife.

Was there, she wondered, burrowing deeper into the blankets, a connection between the two events? And who sat in the crypt with a monk's habit and modern shoes? If a crime had been committed then it was her duty to do something about it, but she fell asleep still wondering what.

SEVEN

✠ ✠ ✠

In the morning the wind had dropped but a fine curtain of needle-sharp rain obscured the loch. Sister Joan, having ventured out to take a look, decided that nobody would be coming over to collect her that day and she might safely remain within and catch up on her examination of conscience.

She was just finishing writing up her conclusions and thinking gloomily that few Daughters of Compassion filled up their notebooks of private faults as fast as she did when she heard from below her name being called.

Going out to the steps she beheld Brother Cuthbert at the foot of them, his aureole of red hair plastered to his head.

"I'm sorry if I'm disturbing you, Sister," he called cheerfully, "but I wondered in case you wanted to come over to the island today."

"In this rain?" She tilted her face skywards and blinked.

"There's a bit of a haar this morning," he agreed, "but Father Abbot thought you might want to work on your painting in the scriptorium seeing the weather's a bit miffish."

"Exceedingly miffish," she agreed wryly, "but how kind of you to come."

"Will you be needing transport then?" he enquired.

At that moment her cave looked temptingly cosy and warm despite its lack of heating, but Brother Cuthbert's kindness ought not to be unrewarded.

"Can you wait a moment or two while I get my things?" she asked.

"Yes, of course. I'll see you at the boat." He turned and plunged down through the pines.

Sister Joan completed her final sentence, shook her head frowningly over the long list of trivial sins that cluttered up her soul, and pulled on her coat. Like her ankle-length habit it was a serviceable grey, with a high collar into which she tucked the ends of her short veil. Prioresses wore a habit of rich purple during their five-year term of office and afterwards a purple ribbon sewn on the sleeve of their grey habit—one for each term during which they had held the post. It wasn't likely, she thought, that she would ever attain to those dizzy heights.

The steps and the slopes below them were slippery with rain. She negotiated them with care and crunched along the shale to where Brother Cuthbert waited, apparently oblivious to the pouring rain.

"I've got the plastic groundsheet for you, Sister," he announced. "It will keep your clothes dry."

"Thank you. This is marvellous." Sister Joan got herself into the boat without wetting her stockings and wrapped herself gratefully into the thick plastic.

"Actually that was a bit of a brainwave of mine," Brother Cuthbert confided, settling vigorously to the rowing. "The plastic's used for corpses until we can get the shrouds sewn."

"Oh dear." Sister Joan looked doubtfully at her shiny covering.

"They're always so much tidier in plastic," Brother Cuthbert said. "At least that's Father Abbot's opinion."

"Do you—is the, er—plastic used very frequently?" she enquired.

"Hardly ever. Monks live to a ripe old age usually— like nuns, I guess. I suppose it's the lack of stress."

"So you haven't witnessed many deaths yourself?" As she asked the question, she wondered if the other would find it a morbid one, but Brother Cuthbert was apparently blessed with a non-analytical mind, answering brightly, "Only old Brother Laurence who was nearly ninety. In a way it's a pity because death is such a splendid affair if one has the right send-off. Don't you think so?"

"I haven't thought much about it. Was Brother Laurence buried in the crypt?"

"Oh no, there haven't been any interments down there for the last couple of hundred years," he replied promptly. "And only abbots were placed there, as a mark of honour, you know."

And the body she had seen fleetingly had been much younger at the time of death than ninety, she reminded herself.

They had reached the further shore and, clutching the plastic which seemed rather less agreeable since she had learned its actual purpose, she clambered ashore and waited while her boatman tied up the small vessel.

"I have to run. Examination of conscience day," he said, joining her. "If you hang the plastic over the end of the wall near the beehives I can get it wiped down before we go back."

"Yes, fine." She spoke somewhat absently, her eyes on the broad, retreating back. What sins would Brother Cuthbert find to confess in the notebook that only the abbot would ever see? She couldn't imagine that anything too serious could ever cloud that lively young soul.

Where the wall dipped low just before the scriptorium she peeled off the clinging plastic, draped it over the stone and went at a run into the building, shivering as she entered. The whole place was probably slightly damp and her imagination sympathized with any long dead monk crouched over his studies with knotted joints complaining at the cold. In their way they had been heroes those long forgotten scribes.

The manuscript had been turned over a page. She walked up and down past it several times.

Sooner or later she would have to go down into the crypt again and take a closer look at the body with the modern shoes on. The thought of doing that was unpleasant no matter how firmly she told herself that death held no intrinsic horror. Only when she was completely satisfied that the matter needed further investigation would she take action of some kind.

Deciding upon a course of action, she thought, was almost as satisfying as carrying it out. With the resolve firmly fixed in her head she took the cloth from the easel on which her picture of the church was fixed and settled down to her work.

The main picture had been done in the sweeping brush strokes she enjoyed. Now the small details—the tiny flowers clustering at the foot of the walls, the sunlight haloing the square tower, the carved gargoyles at each side of the door. She used the smaller brushes for that, standing back every few minutes to observe the effect. She was as near being pleased with what her hand had shaped as she could ever be.

The outer door opened quietly and the tall figure of the abbot came in, paused for a moment, then trod softly towards her.

"Do I disturb you, Sister?" he enquired.

"Of course not, my lord," she began.

But he held up a hand as delicately moulded as an El

Greco, saying, "We never use the formal term of 'my lord' here, Sister. Father Abbot is the only title necessary."

"Father Abbot." She corrected herself with a smile. "I hope that you will be good enough to accept the two paintings of the chapel I'm going to complete while I'm here."

"Good enough?" he echoed, returning her smile. "I consider it a most generous offer and I won't scruple to take advantage of it. May I look? Oh, but you have talent, Sister! The painting has a lovely serene glow about it."

"It won't take very long to finish," she told him. "Then, if you don't mind, I would like to come over for a few more times to work on a companion piece, the church in winter."

"By all means, but won't your own order wish to receive some sample of your work?"

"I hope to paint the retreat as a gift for my own convent," she said.

"Yes, of course." He nodded understandingly, adding with a delicate air of diffidence, "But I trust your artistic work isn't interfering with your spiritual retreat? It is, of course, none of my business."

"I am trying to balance the two, Father Abbot."

"Of course." He nodded again. "We all live between the saddle and the ground. I am sure you young people manage it beautifully. Brother Cuthbert was telling me that he showed you the crypt."

Sister Joan mentally thanked Brother Cuthbert for not having blurted out her trespass, and said demurely, "It was most interesting, Father Abbot. I hope it was all right for me to go down there?"

"In general we don't," the abbot said. "It is important to keep the air as little disturbed as possible down there. My own feeling is rather against such mausoleums; the dead should return to the dust from whence they came in my opinion; however one hesitates to disturb them further. We leave them in peace."

Which means, she thought with a mixture of relief and dismay, that I can scarcely go blundering down there again.

Something of her thought must have shown on her face because the abbot said, "Of course while you are visiting us you must feel free to go down there if you wish to pray or have a period of meditation. To a young girl like yourself with the prospect of dissolution many years ahead it is sometimes a very useful discipline to contemplate it at close quarters."

"Brother Cuthbert would say that I was much closer to my own dissolution than I'd care to admit," Sister Joan said and chuckled.

"Brother Cuthbert," said his superior tolerantly, "is very young for his age—and his age is also young. He is one of the fortunate ones who was called early to the religious life. Have you everything you require here, Sister?"

"Everything, and I am very grateful for your kindness," she assured him.

"I am afraid that you are not likely to receive much hospitality from the local people," he said.

"That's true, but the McKensies have been very obliging." She had taken up her brush again and dabbed sunlight on to a leaf. "Dolly McKensie and her son?"

"Ah yes, the woman whose husband left her and never returned. We get a newspaper here occasionally through the kindness of the parishioners, and at the time there was something about it."

"Things like that aren't usually reported in the Press, are they?"

"I wouldn't have thought so, but Mrs. McKensie

made quite a fuss about it at the time, I understand. Of course I never met the family personally. I am afraid that neither Mr. McKensie nor his son kept up the practice of the faith. There is no local parish priest who might have kept them up to the mark and, of course, it is not for me to seek to mend matters. My only concern must be the community here."

"Did Mrs. McKensie think something had happened to him?"

"She insisted that he would never have walked out with no word of his intention. The truth is that gentlemen are not always gentle when it comes to abandoning a wife. The son still lives with her?"

"He helps out in the shop."

She decided that Rory's loss of faith had been a confidence intended for her alone, not to be divulged to anyone else no matter how well intentioned. And it would only distress the elderly abbot to learn of something about which he could do nothing practical.

"That is good to hear." He looked pleased.

"I also had dinner at the manse," she informed him.

"Do you think that was wise?" He frowned slightly. "I understand the minister is a widower and I do wonder if he knows the respect with which we in the faith regard our religious—and you are still very young."

Sister Joan tried to picture herself as a tempting morsel for the minister to nibble at and choked back a giggle. It was rather flattering in a way, she supposed, but it was also irritating since it seemed to prove that the last bastion of male chauvinism could be found in the monastery.

"Well, I must leave you to your task," he said after a moment. "Today is a fast day for us—Wednesday, but I can have a cup of tea provided for you."

"Water will suit me fine," she assured him. "I ate well at the manse last night. Mr. Sinclair mentioned that

you had invited him here once but that he was obliged
to refuse because of what his congregation might say."

"That was many years ago, just before his wife died.
A very sad accident."

"Her daughter, Morag, resembles her greatly judging
from the portrait I saw," Sister Joan said.

"She acts as housekeeper for her father, I understand?"

"Very efficiently," Sister Joan said dryly.

"Ladies are frequently so, I believe." He gave a dep-
recating little cough and turned away, saying genially as
he departed, "And please feel free to visit the crypt if
you wish. Thank you again for offering me and the
community such a generous gift. We will hang it in a
place of honour, I promise you."

When she had worked another half hour on her painting she laid down her brushes and stood back, head
tilted to examine her work. It wasn't as good as the picture in her head but it would pass muster, with a charm
and warmth about the picture that conveyed the sense of
welcome she had hoped to capture. The companion picture would be the one set in the winter season, with the
church darkly glowing in the imagined snow. She
would use the first study as model for the second one.

Meanwhile there was the crypt to be visited and she
felt a stab of unease at the thought of descending again
into that vault.

"When we feel it our duty to undertake a certain
course of action," her novice mistress had said, "always
be sure that we do not confuse our personal wishes with
our sense of responsibility. Sometimes the two may
march together, but when they do not then duty must always take precedence."

In this case it was certainly no personal desire of her
own that urged her down into the crypt again. If her ob-

servation hadn't been coloured by her imagination then she would have to inform the authorities of her discovery. Once she did that then she would set in motion events that might have far-reaching consequences. At the very least her own spiritual retreat would be set at risk.

She covered the painting and washed her hands in the little washroom. As she left the scriptorium, walking swiftly through the diminishing rain, she glimpsed the disapproving face of the lay brother who had brought her something to eat before. He stood at the kitchen door, frowning out into the dampness, and before she could give him a polite greeting had closed it firmly. Perhaps he enjoyed cooking and found fast days boring or, more likely, was tired of seeing a female about the place.

In the church two brothers knelt in their stall, evidently finishing the penances imposed on them after the general examination of conscience. She went to one of the benches at the other side and knelt down herself, allowing herself the luxury of ten Aves to give the monks time to finish their prayers and leave, and her own heart time to stop thumping.

The soft padding of two pairs of sandalled feet and the closing of a door told her she was alone again. It would have been far pleasanter to linger here, but Brother Cuthbert would be coming to collect her soon, and she wanted to do her small piece of investigation alone.

Rising, she approached the altar, passed within the rail and went into the sacristy. The door was closed but not locked and within all was in order, cassocks and stoles hanging limply along the wall, Prayer Books piled neatly on a shelf. She crossed to the door of the crypt, opened it, and switched on the light.

Not a mote of dust moved in the empty stillness. She went down the stone steps, found and lit the half burnt candle and held it high as she went on along the tunnel until she rounded the corner and came into the vaulted chamber where the long dead abbots sat in lonely contemplation.

"And now to find out," she said under her breath.

She walked forward to where the seated figure was— had been. Her hand shook violently and hot wax from the candle dripped hurtingly on to her flesh as she stared at the empty alcove.

A dead body, no matter how well preserved by the dry air, couldn't just get up and walk away. Her common sense told her that. Which meant that someone had removed it—up the stairs into the church when the rest of the community was occupied elsewhere? Or up the further steps into the enclosure itself? She bent, squatting close to the stone floor, the candle flame picking out the faint scratches as of shoes sliding over the ground. Too faint to constitute proof of anything at all, she thought, and shivered as the electric light went out and her tiny flame became her own defence against the darkness.

She rose fighting down a sudden, completely irrational terror, that if she looked behind her she would see, shadowless in the flickering light, the figure of the robed man in the modern shoes with empty eyesockets glaring.

She turned to face the emptiness she knew was there, and made her way to the wall where the second light switch was, pressing it down and scolding herself for the relief that flooded her.

"If you could only talk."

Even as her lips shaped the wistful thought and her eyes ranged over those other seated figures she felt the last rags of primitive superstition tug at the neat hem of her civilized self.

If one of them were to speak, to point her in a particular direction with skin-shrouded bone fingers—she
crossed herself as a barrier against stupid fears and went
with slow, measured steps towards the tunnel again. She
left the candle on its ledge, blew out the flame, checked
that the light from the bulb would last a little while
longer by pressing down on the switch again, and then
went steadily on up the steps and into the church again.

The body had gone which meant that in practical
terms she had nothing to report. There should have been
relief in that but she felt inside herself the slow burning
of anger. Someone was playing tricks and she suspected
that the tricks were directed at her—or possibly employed to drive her away from the island, to discourage
her curiosity. She knelt down by the altar rail and
buried her face in her hands while thoughts threaded
themselves like beads on a rosary along the loom of her
mind. The body was that of a man who had died fairly
recently—how recently she couldn't possibly tell since
the natural process of decomposition had been arrested;
someone had placed the body in the crypt, reckoning on
its not being noticed among the others since the vault
was so seldom visited; someone had spied on her during
mass and later, when she had waited for the abbot to escort her into the parlour; someone had crept into the
scriptorium and turned the pages of the illuminated
manuscript to the section dealing with the legend of
Black Morag; someone had grasped her hand in the
darkness of the crypt. Someone, someone. But who?

She crossed herself and rose.

Brother Cuthbert was waiting outside, though waiting
which suggested impatience was scarcely applicable to
the cheerful and casual manner in which he leaned
against the wall, his eyes fixed on the grey sky with as

much pleasure as if he beheld a blue one with scudding white clouds.

"I didn't like to interrupt your devotions, Sister," he said as she emerged from the church. "The rain's easing but it might be wise to wrap the plastic around yourself."

"I don't have it, Brother. I left it over the wall near the beehives," she said. "I assumed that you had taken it."

"I had to rush off to examine my conscience," Brother Cuthbert said. "It wasn't on the wall so I thought you'd forgotten it or something."

"No, I draped it over the wall," she repeated. "There wasn't any wind and it was heavy anyway."

"One of the other brothers must have taken it indoors then. Shall I run and find out?"

"A shower of rain won't make me melt," she protested. "Shall we go to the boat?"

"At your service, Sister." He straightened up, took the stalk of grass he had been nibbling out of his mouth and looked at it in some dismay. "Now isn't that just typical of me! Wednesday is always a fast day and there I go, chewing. There are times when I wonder how it is that I can keep the big rules without any problems but the little ones defeat me—not that fasting is unimportant but chewing a bit of grass seems trivial."

"No sin," said Sister Joan primly, "is trivial."

"So Father Abbot says," Brother Cuthbert mourned, looking less cheerful.

"And not all of them are capital offences either," Sister Joan said briskly. They glanced at each other and grinned wryly.

"That's odd." They had reached the boat and he frowned at it.

"What's odd?" she enquired.

"There must have been a wind or something. I tied her up with two knots the way that I always do and now she's only secured by one. See?"

"Can wind untie knots?"

"I wouldn't have thought so, but you never know. But the wind had dropped by this morning anyway."

"Someone took the boat out then."

"I'm the only one who generally does and then it always has to be with Father Abbot's permission."

"Then you forgot and only tied one knot."

"I'm positive I didn't—oh well, it's of no real importance. Let me help you down, Sister."

Helped into the boat she wound her scarf around her head to protect her veil from the spray and tried to answer her companion's occasional remarks sensibly as he rowed her back to the shore. Her thoughts strayed elsewhere.

The body had gone and with it her chance of going to the police—since any tale she told would be regarded as hysterical nonsense. The plastic sheet used to cover corpses until their burial was also gone. Someone had tied up the boat with only one knot instead of two.

"When the examination of conscience takes place," she said cunningly, "I always feel so silly confessing before my sisters. I have such mean little faults— inattention during prayers, speaking before I think about it, not having any patience with people who are slower than me."

"I think you're probably being too hard on yourself, Sister," he demurred. "In our community we don't have general confession except during Lent, so at least we are spared the embarrassment during the rest of the year of knowing that all our stupidities are known to all the others. Four of us are ordained priests so we can make our confession privately—unless one has done something awful like breaking the grand silence which affects the spirituality of the whole monastery."

So it would have been possible for any of the brothers to slip away down to the crypt, to wrap the body in the sheet of heavy plastic and lift it or drag it away—where?

"Do you need some help, Sister?"

She started slightly at his voice, realizing that the boat had scraped against shingle.

"Oh no, thank you, I'm fine. I—er won't be coming over to the island tomorrow, by the way. I need to give the paint time to dry and I need even more to catch up on my devotions. Could you ferry me across again on Friday morning?"

"A pleasure, Sister. Rowing is splendid exercise for me—and Father Abbot tells me that I can take out the boat whenever you need it. Watch your step now. God bless."

"Don't chew any more grass until tomorrow," she warned smilingly as she watched her step and disembarked neatly.

There was a fine mist hanging over the loch. When she glanced back she saw the boat with its muscular occupant like the fragment of a dream.

"God bless," she said absently and turned to crunch her way along the shoreline, thinking sombrely that someone, at least, must be in particular need of blessing.

"Sister, wait a minute!"

She turned as behind her Morag trotted along the beach. For the other wet weather clearly held no terrors. Her long hair was jewelled with sea mist and she wore only thick sweater and breeches that clung damply to her slender frame. Sister Joan had the sudden bizarre notion that girl and horse had just risen up out of the sea.

"I saw the monk rowing you ashore," Morag said, reining in.

"Yes." Sister Joan paused as Morag dismounted, holding out her hand and adding cordially, "And good afternoon. The rain seems to be clearing."

"Aye but there was a haar earlier." The other hesitated, then shook hands briefly and reluctantly, the colour rising in her face as she went on. "Actually I wanted a word. My father thinks I was—off-hand with you the other night. Not welcoming. I promised I'd apologize."

"There really isn't any need." Sister Joan, feeling dreadfully embarrassed, felt her own colour rising in sympathy. "The meal was delightful. I'm jealous of your culinary skills."

"I like cooking." Morag looked pleased. "It was the only thing that I was good at in school. Sometimes I've thought that it might be quite fun to run an hotel but one needs more than a liking for cookery to do that— and it would hardly be the thing, would it? To turn the manse into an hotel?"

"What does your father think?" Sister Joan enquired cautiously.

"My father thinks that I ought to get married." Morag made a little grimace of distaste. "He isn't very sociable anyway. His asking you over was a sop to hospitality, that's all."

"And there was I imagining that he looked forward to my sparkling conversation," Sister Joan said mildly.

Morag bit her lip and gave an unwilling laugh.

"Sorry," she said wryly. "I'm being rude again. No, he does want to lessen local tensions, show that it's possible to believe different things and still get on with one's neighbours."

"But you don't agree?"

"I speak as I find." The sulkiness was back in the other's face. "I know it's childish but there you are."

Sister Joan wondered where precisely "there" was. Morag Sinclair, unlike her father, seemed to have a rooted prejudice against Catholics. Yet it was she who had met the cowled figure, gone with him into the pine wood, and the torn piece of paper with its overheated words of passion had been found in the same place only the next day.

"So, if you feel like coming again, do," Morag said.

"That's very kind of you but this is a spiritual retreat for me, which means cutting down on social activities no matter how tempting," Sister Joan said.

"Well, at least you abide by your own rules," Morag said grudgingly.

"I try. Most people do."

"Not everybody." Morag spoke stonily, turning to remount.

"I'm sorry?" Sister Joan tilted her head.

"Rory McKensie's father, for one," Morag said, averting her own face. "He had no regard for loyalty, did he?"

"His going off and leaving his wife, you mean? We can't judge unless we know all the circumstances, and his wife still hopes that he might come back."

"Dolly McKensie?" Mounted now, Morag looked down at her with angry scorn in her face. "You weren't fooled by that, were you? McKensie's dead and his wife killed him."

Before the other could answer she had dealt her horse a blow on the rump that sent him forward, pieces of shale flying up from beneath his speeding hooves.

EIGHT

✠ ✠ ✠

Sister Joan had adored the reissue of *Gone with the Wind*, and though she couldn't entirely approve of Scarlett O'Hara's moral standards, she had always thought that thinking about a problem later showed good sense though it wasn't advice she found easy to take. Now, however, she squared her shoulders, stared after the retreating rider and said firmly, "I'll think about it tomorrow."

Then she climbed up the slopes to the steps below the cave, fixing her mind firmly on the theme she had chosen to meditate on—the loneliness of sanctity. That dark soul night endured in varying degrees even by those who weren't saints had always chilled her imagination. To feel oneself entirely alone, deserted by one's Creator, must be the most exquisite mental torture. She had known only the greyness of feeling her prayers falter and fall back to earth and even those periods were rare. As a novice she had been convinced that she was undergoing the dark night and had been firmly set right by her novice mistress who had said briskly, "Probably a touch of constipation, Sister. The change in diet often has that effect. Syrup of figs will settle that problem."

Suddenly, achingly, she missed the company of her sisters. She had left the mother house in London more than a year before and been transferred to the Cornish house and while she missed her former prioress, Mother Agnes, she had, in the time since, learnt to appreciate the different qualities of Mother Dorothy, to look forward to the advice handed out by the old nuns in the infirmary, even to smile at Sister Martha's overenthusiastic help at the precise moment it wasn't needed.

She paused at the top of the steps and turned to look over the loch with the rain lifting like a curtain to reveal the sunlit water. This was a beautiful place with a canker at its heart—the remnants of ancient prejudice, suspicion of murder, a vanished husband—not to mention a vanished body, she thought wryly.

All these things flung into her lap at the very time when she had looked forward to tranquillity! She heaved an involuntary sigh, scolding God silently for cluttering up her life with matters exceedingly temporal, and went inside, kneeling on the stone before the bare wall of rock, fitting her mind painfully to the theme of her meditation.

The shadows were lengthening when she rose, rubbing her cramped knees, and deciding that aiming at sanctity was hard on the joints. She was also hungry. A tin of soup heated up with a hunk of bread and a couple of apples would be a feast. She moved to open the heavy door and was immediately hailed by Rory McKensie who stopped halfway up the steps, calling out, "Sister Joan, my mother has asked me to come over and take you back for supper with us. I hope you'll come because she doesn't often have visitors."

"Well, I don't—" Sister Joan hesitated, then nodded. "It's very kind of your mother to think of me and I'd like very much to come."

"I'll wait at the bottom," Rory announced and scrambled down with the agility of a young colt.

She followed more circumspectly, having prudently

put the torch in her bag. Stumbling homeward in the dark wasn't her favourite occupation and it would be foolish to rely on Rory's being gallant. The way in which he had framed the invitation made it very clear that it came from his mother.

"You're quite good on your feet, Sister," he said in reluctant compliment when she joined him.

"For my advanced age, you mean? You and Brother Cuthbert both."

"Brother who?"

"Cuthbert. He also considers me in my dotage."

"And you consider me to be a mere child," he retorted.

"At twenty. Hardly. Anyway years have nothing to do with it. One of the nuns in my own convent is in her eighties and has more youth in her than a dozen teenagers."

"She sounds OK," he said cautiously.

"She is. How nice of your mother to ask me to supper. I warn you that I have a hearty appetite."

"Don't worry. She's used to mine." He grinned suddenly, the dour lines of his face lifting into boyishness. "You went over to the manse last evening."

"I am becoming a gadabout, I fear. Why?"

"You'll have met Morag." He spoke gruffly, averting his gaze.

"Ah yes," Sister Joan said mildly. "The ghostly Black Morag who rides into and out of the loch on her trusty steed, and is incidentally an excellent cook."

"Oh," said Rory, looking somewhat at a loss as if a rebuke he'd been anticipating hadn't materialized.

They were walking through the gully now where the fading light purpled the rock. Sister Joan gave him a level look.

"I wondered why you tried to mislead me," she said

mildly. "Trying to frighten me a little bit with tales of hauntings, I daresay."

"I just didn't want to talk about the present day Morag Sinclair," he said reluctantly. "I can't stand her. She thinks that she and her father own the loch. She's as proud as a peacock with nothing to show for it."

"And you are very attracted to her," Sister Joan said, adding hastily, "Not that it's any of my business, of course."

"I don't want to talk about it," Rory said.

"Naturally not." Sister Joan prepared to mount the steps of the bridge.

"We used to be good friends," Rory said, promptly embarking on the subject he had just eschewed. "Morag's a couple of years older than I am but it never made much difference when we were younger even though I was a Catholic—well, a nominal one and her father was the minister—and then she went off to a boarding-school and it still didn't matter because we used to get together in the holidays. To tell you the truth, at one time, I had the silly idea that I was in love with her—and it didn't matter that my father had done a bunk—run off, I mean. I'd have married her when I was old enough and her father could have conducted the service because I'd lost my faith anyway."

"So you told me." Sister Joan resolved that if he craved disapproval he needn't fish in her direction.

"Anyway it made no difference in the end," Rory said, evidently deciding to throw caution to the winds and speak frankly. "A couple of years ago Morag took against me—told me that she didn't want to see me again—not in the old way, that is. She wouldn't tell me why. Said she'd decided it was a mistake; she wanted to meet other people etcetera, etcetera."

"Surely lots of people feel like that sometimes," Sister Joan said. "I mean a person sometimes needs time apart so they can decide if they really want to stay with their partners. You can't blame Morag for that."

"But she didn't go off to meet other people," Rory said. "She stayed here, keeping house for her father, riding about on that dam—dratted horse of hers as if she owned the neighbourhood. We used to talk about starting a riding stables together one day, perhaps combining it with an hotel—you know treks for tourists and that kind of thing. It would bring more revenue to the loch and the village. She could have gone off and done it by herself or made another career or—she stayed on."

"*La belle dame sans merci* hath me in thrall," Sister Joan said quietly.

"Something like that." He was too young to smile at the quotation.

"Have you ever tried to talk to her about it?" Sister Joan asked.

He shook his head. "I'm not about to go running after someone who thinks I'm just a kid not to be taken seriously," he said. "Anyway you can see why I don't want to talk about it. You won't mention it to my mother? She never had much time for the Sinclairs anyway."

"I won't say a word," she promised gravely.

They were walking up the village street between the shops and cottages. Curtains were already drawn and light beamed through the gaps into the street.

"Hardly the Las Vegas of Scotland, is it?" Rory said, recovering his cheerful manner.

"I suppose people go to bed early here or, at any rate, get within doors?" She glanced at him as the reached the top of the hill.

"There isn't much to do except a bit of night fishing.

We won't have to go through the shop. There's a side door."

He was already pushing it open, ushering her down a passage and up a flight of stairs. At the top of them Dolly McKensie, her overall removed to reveal high-necked sweater and a flared skirt waited with a welcoming smile on a face to which she had applied a touch too much make-up in colours that didn't exactly suit her. The effect was that of a portrait too hastily drawn from which the colours are already beginning to seep.

"I hope you didn't think it cheeky of me to ask you over at short notice?" she said by way of greeting.

"I was delighted to receive the invitation," Sister Joan said.

"Come in then." Dolly held the door wider to allow her guest to pass into a fairly large living-room which evidently stretched over the shop beneath.

The room was comfortably warm with a brightly patterned carpet, a television set which Dolly hurriedly switched off, a three-piece suite piled with cushions and a round table set in formal fashion. The only pictures on view were two Corot prints over the fireplace and, on a small piano in one corner, a large framed photograph of a baby which, Sister Joan guessed, was Rory even before that young man pounced upon it, turning it face down with a reproachful, "Honestly, Mum, I told you to get rid of that. It's embarrassing."

"At least you weren't on a bearskin," Sister Joan said with a grin.

"Take no notice of him, Sister." Dolly sounded faintly overhearty in the manner of many people unused to the conversation of the religious. "Sit down and make yourself comfortable, Sister. I've a nice piece of salmon for supper, so you'll enjoy that."

"Indeed I shall," Sister Joan said, wondering why everybody offered her salmon, and promptly castigating herself for being ungrateful.

"Tinned," said Dolly. "Not that tasteless fresh stuff. And there's a trifle afterwards—is that all right?"

"That's more than all right. It's sinful luxury," Sister Joan said, chuckling.

"It must be getting very cold up in that cave," Dolly continued. "The place wouldn't suit me even in the summer and summer's past."

"Oh, I'm used to roughing it a bit," Sister Joan said, easing herself closer to the edge of the overstuffed chair into which she had been guided.

"It must be terrible," Dolly said, adding vaguely, "Sublimation, you know. Rory, do stop fidgeting about the place and get Sister Joan a glass of sherry. You'll take a glass of sherry?"

"A small one, please."

The sherry was a vintage one. Sister Joan sipped it appreciatively, reminding herself that she hadn't eaten all day and had best take care lest it went to her head. At the rate she was going she'd be the only nun in history to come back from a retreat as a full blown alcoholic.

"Take a seat, Sister, and let me have your coat. Rory, you should have taken Sister's coat," Dolly scolded.

"Sorry." Rory hung it at the back of the door and pulled out a chair at the table.

Thankfully it was a hard chair. Sister Joan allowed her hostess to serve her with the bright pink salmon and the inevitable salad and new potatoes. Rory, looking ill at ease, had sat down at her other side and Dolly took her place with a brightly tinkling little laugh.

"Isn't this nice!" she said. "Not as grand as the manse, of course, but there—"

"Mother." Rory's voice was warning. Dolly glanced at him, bit her lip, and subsided.

"I always think that the company matters more than the surroundings," Sister Joan said, jumping in with both feet.

"And the Sinclairs aren't exactly matey—no, Rory, it's true. Mr. Sinclair has kept himself to himself for as long as I can remember and his daughter thinks she's better than the rest of us put together—"

"Have some bread, Sister," Rory broke in. "Salt?"

"Just bread, thank you." Sister Joan took a piece.

"So how are you getting on up there then?" Dolly asked with an air of reluctantly changing the subject.

"Very well," Sister Joan said, "and the exercise I'm getting from climbing up and down is doing wonders for my figure."

"Oh, do you worry about that sort of thing?" Dolly looked surprised. "I wouldn't have thought it mattered, your being a bride of Christ or whatever they call it."

"It's healthier to be slim," Sister Joan said, "and I've never understood why Our Blessed Lord should be saddled with all the fat, plain women."

Dolly gave her a shocked stare but Rory let out a guffaw, exclaiming, "You see, Mum, she's just like a real person!"

"Could a real person have another slice of bread?" Sister Joan enquired. The bread came from a sliced commercial loaf and was tasteless enough to offset the too rich sauce in which the salmon was smothered.

They progressed to the trifle which was unexpectedly good.

"Well, I'll be off then." Rory was suddenly on his feet.

"What about Sister?" his mother asked.

"I'll be back in half an hour. I promised to help out

with Jimmy's bike. You don't have to rush, do you?"
He looked at Sister Joan.

"As long as I'm not too late—but I have a torch—the
one I bought from your shop, as a matter of fact," Sister
Joan remembered, "so I can easily take myself home if
you're delayed."

"I'll try to get back." Rory ignored his mother's
frown and went out, taking his anorak from behind the
door as he left.

"Coffee or tea, Sister? I favour a nice cup of tea after
salmon, don't you?" Dolly said, bustling her visitor
back to the armchair.

"A cup of tea is always welcome." Sister Joan hoped
she would be able to lever herself up out of the chair
when it was time to leave.

"I just hope Rory hasn't gone down to the loch."
Dolly spoke restlessly, bringing in the tea. "I know he's
past twenty and shoulders a lot of responsibility for his
age but when a boy gets crazy ideas about a girl—
woman, I ought to say—that one never was a girl! Born
ancient she was—like her mother."

"Catherine Sinclair, would that be? I saw her portrait
when I was at the manse," Sister Joan said mildly. "She
looked very like her daughter."

"In more ways than one, Sister." Dolly snapped her
lips together.

Sister Joan drank the tea that had been pressed upon
her. She had a distinct feeling of being pulled in two di-
rections at once. She wanted to leave before she was
forced to listen to what she feared might be some very
unpleasant gossip; she wanted to stay because somewhere in the other's bitter words might be some clue to
the accusation that Morag had flung over her shoulder
and possibly to the elusive body in the crypt.

"Mind you," Dolly said after a moment, "I must be

fair. Backaways, when they were children, Morag and
Rory used to get along fine for all that we're shopkeep-
ers and he's clergy—and don't say it doesn't signify. In
rural areas it signifies all right—but with those two it
didn't seem to matter, and the Sinclairs for all their airs
never had two pennies to rub together. And I never in-
terfered between the two of them, not even when
Alasdair—that's my husband—took off. Not that I believe he did—not for a minute. I told the police that
he'd not leave without letting me know. They said he'd
given up his job and sold his car and it was clear he
meant to disappear—and I can't pretend I wasn't glad
in some ways to see the rear end of him because he'd
never been the cherishing kind—but that didn't mean I
wasn't entitled to have a search made, now did it?"

"And nothing was found?" Whatever her private res-
ervations it looked as if she were impelled to listen.

"Not one trace," Dolly said with a curious mixture of
triumph and regret.

"I suppose," said Sister Joan, feeling her way carefully, "that adults are entitled to—disappear and, if
there's no evidence of a possible crime, there's nothing
the police can do. It must have been very difficult for
you."

"Not as difficult as being married," Dolly said.
"Alasdair was well enough when we first wed. He was
proud of having a son but he never took a close interest
in his rearing. Nor in his religion either. He was usually
away at weekends anyway so he never went over to the
island for mass. There were other women, I'm certain
of that."

"You knew about them?"

"Guessed. You see, Sister, after Rory was born
Alasdair hardly ever touched me—in that way, if you
follow my meaning. So there was another woman

somewhere. A man can't serve two at once and satisfy them both."

Sister Joan felt herself wince slightly at the crudity, but merely nodded as if she knew all about such situations.

"And I can tell you something else," said Dolly.

Her tongue had been loosened so thoroughly that Sister Joan wondered fleetingly if there was something stronger than tea in the other's cup, but it seemed more likely that Dolly McKensie, starved of a confidante, was simply unburdening herself which meant that when she thought back over the conversation later she would be extremely embarrassed and withdraw from any further contact with her guest.

"Perhaps you had better think," she said gently, "before you make so intimate a confidence—one often regrets speaking—"

"Alasdair," said Dolly, breaking in impatiently, "was seeing Catherine Sinclair."

"My dear Mrs. McKensie, you can't possibly—"

"Do you think I didn't guess who was occupying his attention?" Dolly said bitterly. "Oh, he was very clever about it—went off in connection with his work so often that we got used to his never being here. I thought for a long time that it was some woman in Argyll—he spent holidays there as a boy—and then I figured out it must be someone nearer—in Aberdeen perhaps. Well, for all I know he had his lovers staked out all over Scotland, but one of them was nearer still. Someone mentioned they'd seen his car near the manse—it was said innocently—oh, you'll be wanting to get off and make the supper for your Alasdair. I saw his car the other side of Loch Morag, near the manse—and me smiling and nodding and thinking all the time that he wasn't due home until the next day."

"He might have been visiting Mr. Sinclair, the minister."

"That weekend the minister had gone down to see the daughter at her boarding-school," Dolly said tightly.

"You're sure of that?"

"There was a notice up, saying that there'd be no service at the kirk that Sunday. It was in the post office. And his wife wasn't going with him. She'd had the flu—I know that because I'd a bit of a cold myself and when I went into MacGregors' to get something for it the assistant mentioned that it did seem to be going round since Mrs. Sinclair had had a bad dose of it. So she was alone in the house and Alasdair's car was outside."

"Did you ask him about it?"

"I'd not give him the satisfaction of thinking what he chose to do bothered me," Dolly said resentfully. "And it wasn't just that. She was in his car. When he did come home I smelled perfume in it. Alasdair may not have been very keen on getting into bed with me, but he was not female in himself. It was as much as I could do to get him to use aftershave."

"I don't think that constitutes proof of his sexual orientation," Sister Joan objected.

"Well, he didn't wear perfume anyway whatever the reason," Dolly said, "and Catherine Sinclair did. She came into the shop once or twice to buy things and she was wearing it then, heavy and musky. And that same perfume was in the car when Alasdair came home."

She ended on a triumphant note, folding her hands together. Sister Joan sipped her tea which had cooled and cast a surreptitious glance at the fob watch pinned to her habit. The evidence for an affair between Alasdair McKensie and Catherine Sinclair seemed tenuous in the extreme, but Dolly clearly felt some satisfaction in having ferreted out the truth as she believed. Perhaps it was easier for her to pin the blame on a known face rather than torment herself with faceless possibilities.

"You must have suffered great anguish of mind," she said at last, seeking safety in the bland, familiar phrase.

"I'd made up my mind to divorce him," Dolly said. "There wasn't anything left between us—no quarrelling, no making up, nothing. I wanted my own independence—seeing to the shop, helping Rory get into a decent career—but he ran off before I could bring the subject up."

She hadn't meant to involve herself even verbally but at this last couldn't avoid exclaiming, "But Catherine Sinclair died, did she not? He couldn't have gone off with her."

"She wasn't the only one," Dolly said. "The one nearest home but not the only one. There must have been others. That was what they must have quarrelled about—"

"You know they quarrelled?"

Dolly looked irritated. "I don't know anything for certain," she said. "I've had time to work it out—six long years. Alasdair disappeared and three weeks later Catherine Sinclair was found dead—an overdose of sleeping tablets. They said it was an accident, and I didn't get to thinking about it for ages. Then Rory and the daughter started seeing each other again—Morag left school and came to housekeep for her father, and then I started thinking again—the smell of her perfume in the car, Alasdair's going off—"

"You think he left Catherine Sinclair and went off with some other woman?"

"If he could cheat on me he could cheat on her too,"

Dolly said. "I reckon he did and she brooded about it and then killed herself. It makes sense."

It would have made better sense, Sister Joan reasoned, if Dolly had been struck by this theory when her husband first disappeared and Catherine Sinclair died. That she had waited six years before drawing her conclusions argued that the intensifying of the relationship between her son and Catherine's daughter had roused her to find some reason to separate them. That all this had probably taken place on her subconscious level was immaterial. Dolly McKensie had craved for a son to rear, not a husband to cherish. Her motives were sadly mixed.

"What are your future plans?" she enquired aloud.

"In a year's time I can apply to the courts to assume my husband is dead. I want to make sure of getting my widow's pension when the time comes," Dolly said. "I've spoken to my lawyer and he doesn't see any difficulty."

"Do you think he is still alive?" Sister Joan asked bluntly.

"Alive and hugging himself for fooling everybody," Dolly said. "He always had a funny sense of humour."

"It must have been terrible for Catherine Sinclair if what you think is true."

"Because she killed herself? Weak-willed, I'd call it. She committed adultery, didn't she?"

There was no use in pointing out that there wasn't a shred of real evidence to prove that, Sister Joan thought. Dolly McKensie had brooded over the matter and, at the precise time when it looked as if her son was seriously interested in another woman, she had drawn her conclusions.

"Did you? Did you mention your ideas—suspicions to anyone?" she asked instead.

"There wasn't any need," Dolly said. "Young Morag threw Rory over without any help from anybody. Thought she was too good for him. He's better off without her, I think."

Rory evidently thought differently. For him Morag's changed attitude had been hurtful and not opportune.

"I hope everything works out well in the end," she said aloud, managing to rise from the capacious chair and only too aware that her comment was banal. "I wish I could think of something more useful to say, but I'll certainly remember you in my prayers. If you don't object to that?"

"I'd do a bit of praying myself," Dolly said, "if I thought it'd do any good. You're not going? Rory won't be long."

"If I know anything about young men once they get their heads under a motorbike time ceases to exist," Sister Joan said. "I shall enjoy the walk and I do have the torch."

"It's been nice talking to you," Dolly said, lifting down the grey coat from the back of the door. "I don't talk about it very much—in fact hardly ever. Hope I haven't bored you?"

"I'm only sorry I can't be of more practical help," Sister Joan said. "I wouldn't give up hope of a solution either if I were you. If your husband is still alive someone somewhere will recognize him—if not something will be found about that too."

"He's not likely to be dead," Dolly said watching her guest put on her outdoor garments. "Mind you, I'll stand up in any court and swear that I believe that I'm a widow. But Alasdair's alive. There's times I can almost feel him laughing at me because he's fooled me and run off."

"Did he take any money with him?" She had no right to enquire but asked anyway.

"He gave me housekeeping from his job as salesman and I kept the profits of the shop. He might have had savings but I don't know where. If he had he's probably bought a snug little bar in Spain and he's living there with his latest bimbo."

"Bimbo?"

"Empty-headed blonde—page three girl—slang."

"In the convent we are apt to miss out on the latest slang," Sister Joan said apologetically. "It's a very interesting word—bimbo. Well, may I thank you most sincerely for my supper. I am disgracefully fond of trifle. And tell Rory not to worry about being late. I like walking by moonlight."

As she had expected the other made no attempt to detain her further. In a little while she would be regretting her indiscretion.

Outside the lamps cast a yellow glow over the steep, cobbled street with its curtained windows and shuttered shop front. The rain had stopped but the air was thick with curling spirals of mist that rose up beneath a sky lit by the barest sliver of moon.

Walking might help to calm the turbulence of her thoughts. Dolly McKensie was not, after all, the grieving widow, hoping for an absent husband to return. She was a woman who wanted her widowhood to be established by law, who had not even liked her husband very much—a host of shabby little deceits must have killed all her loving. Sadder still was her fixation on the dead Catherine Sinclair as the woman in the case. With no concrete evidence at all, Sister Joan reminded herself. But Dolly McKensie had found the belief a convenient one when it became clear that her son was in love with Catherine's daughter. How relieved she must have felt when her plans to separate them were anticipated by Morag's own actions, because Morag Sinclair believed that Dolly McKensie had killed her husband.

Reaching the bottom of the street Sister Joan paused to collect her thoughts and switch on her torch.

Morag had decided to drop Rory because she believed his mother was a killer. She obviously hadn't voiced the real reason for her rejection and both Dolly and Rory had reached the conclusion that she had decided she could do better for herself. But had Morag based her own belief on anything substantial or was she too leaping to conclusions? And why would Morag believe him to be dead?

It was no use. She had tried to push away her memory of that seated figure with the modern shoes under the hem of the black habit. He returned, filling the canvas of her mind. Where better place to conceal a body than among other bodies? Which meant that Dolly McKensie could have put it there?

Sister Joan crossed the bridge and started down the gully, her torch making a broad pathway of light before her. By contrast the surroundings looked blacker. As she turned on to the shoreline she hesitated, then switched off the torch. The unnecessary use of a battery was not compatible with a vow of poverty. And the sliver of moon had been joined by stars and the wind was ruffling the mist into trailing ribbons of grey. She stood for several moments, letting her eyes become accustomed to the gloom, and then walked on steadily, her feet crunching the shale.

On her right the water was a darkly shining expanse. On her left the cliffs reared up high, crowned with bare rock off which the starlight glanced. The pines leaned a little, stretching towards the loch, their trunks faintly gleaming.

The soft plashing of water lifted by oars came to her ears. She stopped, her feet slithering on the little wet pebbles, and saw the boat approaching, the cowled figure bent over his task like some faceless Charon traversing the Styx.

Not everybody in the monastery enclosure slept that night. She waited as the plashing of water gave place to scraping. The boat had grated against the pebbles that littered the shore to the water's edge. The cowled figure was seated there, holding the craft almost motionless, head bent.

Sister Joan had reached the place below the steps to the cave. She turned and climbed softly as a cat up the steep path that wound between the gleaming pines, not wanting—not daring—to look down and see anything more.

When she reached the cave she stumbled within, switching on the torch again, her heart beating fast. What was happening had about it the unreal quality of someone else's bad dream into which she, unwittingly, had strayed by mistake.

NINE

☩ ☩ ☩

"And what," said Sister Joan, sitting back on her heels and looking up vaguely in the direction where most people envisage God as sitting, "am I supposed to do? This is a spiritual retreat, Lord, designed to enhance my inner strength and here I am being dragged into someone else's problem again. What am I to do?"

The Creator appeared to be silent this morning. If He had had as fitful a sleep as herself she thought it very likely that He was having a lie-in.

During the night she had tossed and turned on the hard, narrow bed, the bitter words of Dolly McKensie echoing in her mind, the things she herself had seen replaying themselves like an old film over and over again in her mind. Sundry unconnected events had, she was certain, some common linkage. The cowled figure who rowed across the loch late in the evening, the body that had vanished from the crypt, the torn-off portion of what was clearly a love letter caught in the tree, Morag's belief that Dolly had killed her husband, Dolly's belief that the said husband had been having an affair with Catherine Sinclair—somewhere they were all joined in what Sister Joan feared was an unholy union.

She had been on her knees since before five and not a whisper of advice or comfort had come from anywhere.

"When it seems that we receive nothing in answer to our prayers," her novice mistress had said once, "then we can be sure we are being tested. The soul must rise to sanctity without constant mollycoddling from heaven."

"A bit of heavenly mollycoddling wouldn't come amiss just now," she muttered, rising and leaning to extinguish the last feeble flame of the burnt-out candle.

Since there evidently wasn't going to be any then she was thrown back on her own sadly inadequate resources. And that, she thought, deciding that any action was better than none, meant a visit to the manse. Morag had made her accusation surely in the knowledge that she would be expected to explain it; she too felt the need to confide in a stranger.

The rain still hung heavily on the air like a curtain of tiny droplets. The waters of the loch were ruffling up indignantly under the onslaught of the rising wind. Above the curtain of waiting rain the sky was a strange gun-metal grey, brooding, powerful. Sister Joan looked at it uneasily. She could feel the threat of storm running along her nerves. Sister Andrew would call this migraine weather. A good brisk walk would make her feel better, she decided, and warm her chilled hands and feet. She put on her coat, wrapped the heavy grey scarf over her veil, and picked up her bag. Descending the slippery steps and the pine clad slope she turned to the right. It would take, she reckoned, a couple of hours to walk right round the loch to the manse. That ought to give the Creator time to decide if He wanted her to talk to Morag or not. If not then Morag wouldn't be in.

Having placed the final responsibility firmly back in heaven she felt more cheerful. Walking was a splendid antidote to depression—not, she told herself hastily, that she was depressed. It was only that the demands of the outer world sometimes weighed a little heavily.

She crossed the bridge and continued walking, skirting the hill over which the village sprawled and taking the track that curved back towards the water. There were no fishing boats out this morning but she could see nets strung out over the low walls behind which a row of small, whitewashed cottages were set. A woman whom she recalled having seen at mass waved from her doorway and raised Sister Joan's spirits even higher. Not everybody here had a rooted prejudice against nuns or a secret to conceal. She waved back and went on, the row of cottages diminishing as she left them behind. She felt warmer now but an ominous growling in her stomach reminded her that she had forgotten to eat any breakfast. She hoped that Morag would be in a hospitable mood but with the minister's daughter there was never any telling what particular mood that young woman would be in.

She had rounded the top of the loch where it narrowed into rocks and a profusion of small waterfalls. She stood for a few moments, looking up at the fine spray which mingled with the mist and then flowed into the boulder strewn bed. There was a narrow railed path which avoided the downpour and took her on to the facing shoreline. The beach was narrower at this side, sloping up abruptly to a gravelled road bordered by massive trees whose exposed roots clung to the thin soil. The road was deserted and only a few dilapidated looking buildings were to be seen strung out along the shore. Further on she could see the wharf and the tangle of masonry and barbed wire that blocked access to the island.

She had reached the terraces below the grey house. Her legs were aching; when she went to teach at the moorland school she rode Lilith, the amiable pony of whom she had grown extremely fond. Riding Lilith struck her now as a most desirable alternative to plodding along.

"For heaven's sake, you never walked all the way round!" The exclamation came from Morag who had just emerged from the front door and was staring down at her.

"And I wasn't even sponsored," Sister Joan quipped, tilting her head to bring into focus the tall girl in the thick sweater and ethnic styled skirt with its wide bands of embroidery.

"A sense of humour, no less," Morag called down. "You'd better come in."

Sister Joan mounted the terraces gratefully.

"If you wanted to see my father he's out for the day," Morag said. "I'm joining him this afternoon—monthly trip to Aberdeen. He has a committee meeting this morning so I begged off. I'll drive in later. Father went on the early train."

"Do you go shopping in Aberdeen?" Sister Joan asked, passing into the cold shadowed hall.

"Sometimes. They have marvellous woven garments there, and sometimes I go to the cinema and sometimes I wander round the art galleries. It makes a change. In here."

She had opened the sitting-room door and was ushering Sister Joan within. To the latter's pleasure a fire blazed in the hearth and a pot of coffee stood at the side with an array of mugs.

"I'm just having a snack. I never bother with breakfast," Morag said. "Will you have something?"

Side dishes held toast, scrambled eggs, and mushrooms. Sister Joan nodded her thanks, blushing as her stomach rumbled again.

"Help yourself. I generally eat here when Father's away," Morag said. "It's cosier than the dining-room. Don't you eat breakfast either?"

"I forgot."

Morag glanced at her and uttered a short laugh. "You forgot to eat breakfast before you set out on a six-mile walk? You must have been very anxious to get here."

"I wasn't very anxious to get here at all," Sister Joan said frankly, sitting down with her food. "I don't mean that quite the way it sounds—I am pleased to find you in. At least I think I am. Oh dear, I'm not expressing myself very well. Look, I'd be happy to be here if I didn't feel obliged to ask you what you meant when you said that Dolly McKensie had killed her husband."

"Did I really say that?" Morag raised innocent eyes.

"And for a reason." Sister Joan felt impatience bubble in her. "Miss Sinclair—Morag, you can't toss a remark like that into the air and not expect to be asked about it. If you haven't any evidence to back up your statement then it's slander, and if you do have good reason then you ought to go to the police or the Sheriff."

"It isn't slander if it's true," Morag said, "and one day I might be in a position to prove it. Of course Dolly McKensie killed him."

"How do you know?" Sister Joan enquired.

"Because—" Morag hesitated, then laid down her knife and fork, crossed to the door and closed it firmly. "Jeannie's in the kitchen," she said, returning, "but I don't want her to overhear anything. She might say something to Father and he's the one person who mustn't know."

"Oh dear," Sister Joan said softly.

"My mother," Morag said tensely, "was having an affair with Alasdair McKensie. Six years ago when I was away at school—doing A Levels and looking forward to the jolly old hols she was—with Dolly McKensie's husband."

"You knew that for certain?"

"No, of course I didn't—not then. Not until a couple of years ago," Morag said impatiently.

"Your mother died—a tragic accident."

"My mother killed herself," Morag said grimly. "Oh, nobody even suspected it at the time. She didn't leave a note the way people usually do, and if she hadn't been run down after a dose of flu the tablets she took wouldn't have hurt her at all. The Coroner reckoned she'd taken the prescribed number of tablets to help her sleep, woke up later, forgotten she'd already taken them and swallowed more. And she'd had a hot toddy to soothe her throat just before she went to bed."

"Didn't your father . . . ?" Sister Joan stopped, feeling acutely uncomfortable.

"He was sleeping in one of the spare bedrooms because of the flu infection. He sometimes did that when he had a long sermon to prepare or a meeting to attend. He left her to sleep in but when she hadn't rung her bell by ten o'clock he went up to make sure she was all right—and found her. He brought me home after the inquest for the funeral and I simply refused to go back. He couldn't get his act together without Mother."

"Then surely it happened as the Coroner found," Sister Joan said. "The whisky in the hot toddy will have increased the effect of the tablets and it is very unwise to keep sleeping tablets by the bed. You have no reason to suppose that she took her own life, have you?"

"I'm trying to tell you," Morag said angrily, her face flushing. "She had a lover—I didn't realize it at the time but much later on I began to remember how different she was during that last holiday. I came home from school and she was—she was always pretty, but that

last summer she was beautiful. She glowed. She was
sometimes sharp in her manner but that summer she
was gentler, dreamy. I was still friendly with Rory then
and I used to feel a bit guilty sometimes because we'd
go off together all day fishing and rock climbing and
riding—we planned to start a stud farm when we'd finished school. Mother didn't say one word about my
neglecting her to run off with my friend and that wasn't
like her; she enjoyed having everybody's attention focused on her. But she never even seemed to notice that
I wasn't there half the time."

"She realized you were growing up."

"She didn't empathize with other people as a rule,"
Morag said. "She was—self-centred. Father never saw
it, of course, because he loved her so much that everything she did was perfect in his eyes."

"But they were happy together, surely?" Sister Joan
said.

"They were happy but she was never radiant when
Father was with her. It was different that last summer.
I sensed the difference but I was so busy with my own
affairs that I didn't analyse the reason for it. And then
I went back to school and just before the next vacation
the headmistress sent for me and told me there'd been
an accident—I took it as such. I really did. And then a
couple of years ago . . ." She stopped abruptly, leaning
to pour more coffee for them both.

Sister Joan sat very still. It was too late to dam up the
flood of confidences—confidences which she had invited by coming here, but at the same time she was
ashamed to find in herself a dreadful curiosity that
needed to be satisfied.

"Father asked me if I'd go through Mother's things,"
Morag said, resuming her seat. "Her clothes had been
given to Oxfam—she was smaller and more rounded

than I am so I could never wear anything of hers, but there were books and letters from old friends and her diaries—she always wrote up her diary."

"You read them, I suppose?"

"She was dead," Morag said defensively, "but in any case there might have been an address she had scribbled down—some old friend who might not have been told she was dead. Anyway I skimmed through everything, and then I found the diary entries for the summer just before she—died. Very brief entries. Meeting A. Ten o'clock. Memo, leave back door on latch. That kind of thing."

"But surely your father's name is Alexander—A."

"Why on earth would she need to remind herself in a diary that she was going to meet her own husband?" Morag demanded sensibly.

"I—suppose not," Sister Joan said unhappily.

"Anyway I checked my father's appointment book when he was out," Morag said, "and on every occasion she'd written 'Meeting A' then he had a meeting or a service elsewhere. And on the day of the night she died that same entry was scrawled, 'Meeting A. Ten o'clock.' Father was out that evening, sitting with an old lady who'd been very sick. He got home at about eleven and he and Mother had a hot toddy together before she went up to bed."

"You didn't tell him—ask him about the entries in the diary?"

Morag shook her dark head.

" 'A' could have been anyone, not necessarily a lover," Sister Joan said.

"I asked Jeannie if my mother had gone out at all during that last evening," Morag said jerkily. "She told me that she'd gone for a stroll around nine o'clock, and come in again just before eleven, saying it was cold."

"And you think she went to meet this person she refers to in her diary?"

"It figures, doesn't it?" Morag said. "And then I remembered that Dolly McKensie's husband had gone missing though she thought he was working away and didn't get round to reporting it for a week or two. He was always swanning off and leaving her and Rory by themselves."

"And your mother planned to go with him but changed her mind? That is another possible explanation," Sister Joan said. "If she really loved your father and you, why she very probably thought better of her impulse."

"And he went off by himself?"

"They both thought better of it."

"If my mother had ever got to the point of deciding to run off with another man she wouldn't have changed her mind because of what it might do to me or my father," Morag said. "She was self-centred, I told you. No, I think that she went to meet Alasdair McKensie and found him dead—or while they were together his wife came along and killed him. I don't know. I do know that they were both connected—and don't think I haven't tried to think of some other explanation. But there isn't any, Sister. One day some little piece of information will slot into place and show that Dolly McKensie killed her husband and my mother killed herself because of what she'd caused to happen."

"So you broke off your friendship with Rory," Sister Joan said.

"How could I go on seeing him when my mother had been having an affair with his father and more than likely his mother was a killer?" Morag asked. There was an unutterable weariness in her voice.

"Why have you told me all this?" Sister Joan asked.

"In the beginning you seemed so hostile though we'd never met—"

"Because I haven't any time for Catholics," Morag interrupted. "Alasdair McKensie was one and he was a bad husband and a neglectful father and when I found out he'd been playing around with my mother—"

"You've found out nothing of the sort." Recognizing incipient hysteria she spoke firmly. "Your mother was meeting someone whose name began with the letter A. There must be hundreds of people in Scotland with that initial. And his vanishing at about the same time your mother died isn't proof of anything either. And as for imagining that his wife followed them and killed him— Morag, use your common sense. Is she likely to have killed him and then left your mother free to return to the manse and possibly telephone the police? It really falls apart when you look at it sensibly, now doesn't it?"

"I've a feeling about it," Morag said obstinately.

"Even if you're right it isn't evidence. Morag, did you think that I was going to start asking questions on your behalf? Stirring up things when there are no grounds for doing so? Or were you expecting me to break into the McKensie home and look for evidence?"

"I don't know what I was expecting," Morag said. "Maybe I just wanted to talk to someone uninvolved, to test out my theory."

"Which isn't a very sound one," Sister Joan said. "I'll regard everything you surmised to me as a confidence to be kept strictly between ourselves. If you want some advice you'd be wise to let the past alone—you can't change anything, and you might cause great misery if you start meddling. And I don't see what any of this has to do with your and Rory's friendship—you're neither of you responsible for what your parents might have done."

"Did Rory mention me at all?" Morag asked.

"Rory McKensie talks to nuns as little as possible," Sister Joan evaded.

"Not," said Morag, "that it bothers me in the least. His mother never liked me very much anyway. One day I'll find out the truth about her."

"What about your father?" Sister Joan looked at her. "I take it that he is unaware that your mother's death might—just might—not have been an accident. He would be greatly grieved if he ever discovered that she might have been involved with another man."

"I know." Morag's face had darkened. "He adored Mother; he never could see the smallest fault in her. But if a crime was committed then is it right to let the criminal go free simply to avoid causing hurt?"

"I believe mercy ranks above justice," Sister Joan said slowly. "Even if someone escapes human justice eventually they will have to face a reckoning."

"That wouldn't give me the same satisfaction," Morag said.

"Think about it as objectively as you can," Sister Joan urged. "Don't rush into anything. Once you start something it's very hard to stop it."

She felt that she had been less than helpful, but Morag was evidently determined to be polite and murmured something indeterminate.

"You will want to be starting on your car trip," Sister Joan said, rising. "And I must start back myself. The brunch was very welcome."

"I can run you back," Morag offered, then glanced at her wrist-watch and uttered an exclamation. "Hell, no! I can't. I promised to pick up some books that Father ordered in Glenloch higher up the hill and the shop closes before one. Look, the boat's moored at the landing-stage. Use that if you know how to row. I have to go. I can collect the boat tomorrow some time. We don't use it that often."

"But your father uses it?"

"He rowed you back the other night, didn't he? Instead of driving you, you mean? The truth is that we both dislike cars. I'd ride Rob Roy all the way to Aberdeen if I could—and my father likes the boat. Maybe we can talk another time?"

Her voice was suddenly young and wistful.

"Yes, of course," Sister Joan spoke as warmly as she could. The truth was that she needed some time by herself to sort out her own complicated feelings about the events taking place around her. The problem of how far to get involved was a difficult one.

"Thank you again. I'll see myself out," she said and went briskly to the door. When she glanced back Morag was biting her lip, her expression troubled. Clearly she had wanted advice and equally clearly she wasn't sure if she wanted to take it.

And what advice could I possibly give? Sister Joan thought, making her way down the terraces. Morag believed that her mother had been having an affair with Alasdair McKensie, a belief which she shared unknowingly with Dolly. But Dolly had given it as her opinion that her husband had run off with some unknown woman and Morag had convinced herself on no evidence at all that Dolly McKensie had made away with Alasdair. Or had both of them sought to confide in a stranger to divert some possible suspicion from themselves?

She crossed the gravel road towards the wharf, reaching it just as with a screech of brakes a small car swooped down a narrow alley at the side of the manse. Morag slowed down long enough to wave and then speeded up again.

Sister Joan went on to the wharf, feeling a small anticipatory glow of pleasure when she saw the boat bobbing there. It was years since she had rowed a boat and she had never pretended to herself that some rowing team was the worse for not having her as a member, but to be alone and in control of her own small vessel promised a short period of enjoyment.

She stepped down into the boat and cast off, reaching for the oars and feeling the unaccustomed strain on her muscles as she pulled away from the land.

Though it was scarcely past high noon she was glad of her coat and scarf, the sun having hidden behind the leaden greyness of the clouds. Yet the breeze that had dispersed the earlier mist had quieted and the water was like smooth grey silk.

She rowed steadily for several minutes, the island on her right gliding past like some imagined Camelot. She could make out the square tower of the church and the long walls enclosing the beehives and the vegetable plots. Overhead a curlew swooped low, uttering a long, sweetly piercing cry. She tilted her head and whistled back, wondering whether the cry had been greeting or warning. Animals sometimes sensed the future before human beings did.

She rested the oars, letting the boat drift a little, her eyes idly scanning the loch. Solitude in the midst of silence calmed her agitated thoughts. She was glad that Morag, having stated her case, had decided she was in a hurry and offered the boat. Out here problems seemed far away. Closing her eyes, she gave herself up to the peace of the moment.

The sky split open, the lead becoming purple and the absent sun fleeing further as lightning tore a jagged line down the horizon. Sister Joan's eyes flew open and she hastily grasped the oars again, bracing herself for the inevitable downpour of rain. It had, surely, to rain.

The sky had blackened now and the waters of the loch reflected nothing. There was a creeping coldness rising about her, blotting out feeling and another cat-claw of lightning made her jump nervously. The further shore was no more than a faint blur.

"At least I know where I'm headed," she said aloud to cheer herself up, and bore down more vigorously on the oars, frowning at their sluggish progress through the dark water.

She might be able to row, she decided, a moment later, but her steering left a lot to be desired. As far as she could tell she had drifted a good distance past the place where she'd aimed to land. She cast a swift look over her shoulder and saw that the island was nearer than she had supposed. In this freak storm it would make better sense to land there and seek shelter. She changed direction and rowed steadily, feeling as if she were moving through syrup so slow was her speed.

Below the loud groaning of the thunder and the crackling of lightning as it aimed downwards towards the loch there was another sound. She became aware of it by degrees—a sucking, pulsating noise as if some gi-ant pump were emptying the loch. She shipped the oars for a moment to listen more attentively, to peer through the increasing darkness and suddenly both she and the boat were caught and lifted and whirled like a cork-screw. Startled she gripped the side of the boat and hung on grimly as it tilted first one way and then the next and one of the oars slipped over into the water and fell down into the blackness.

"Hail Mary, full of grace . . ." The well-loved words came jerkily, impelled for the first time in her life by fear and not devotion.

The sucking sound again as if all the waters in the world were being siphoned off and, as the whirlpool lifted the little craft and spun it round a final time, the sight, gleaming weirdly under another forked spray of brilliant white light, of a row of heads, ancient and knotted, facing her as they rose up to bar her way.

Not heads, she realized suddenly, but the tops of the polled and fossilized trees that were only revealed when there was a freak tide. To be able to find a rational explanation for her situation made her feel less at the mercy of a pitiless uncaring nature. She was half lying across the bows, the remaining oar trapped beneath her shoulder. The boat was scudding now straight to the drowned trees. She risked moving, seizing the oar, the little vessel tilting alarmingly as she tried to wriggle upward again. If she could reach the trees she could secure the boat and wade to the island before the water rushed in again.

She struck out fiercely, her mouth compressed with determination. She had no particular fear of death though she suspected that the dying might be rather distressing, but at thirty-six she had a lot of living still to do. Well, close on thirty-seven, she admitted to herself. Still young—a mere baby in the eyes of Father Abbot.

The nearest tree trunk was within reach but the waters were boiling coldly, as the dreadful sucking noise threatened her. She had a length of rope in her hand with no clear idea of when she had taken it up. If she could attach it to some projection on the tree trunk then she could scramble ashore somehow.

The wet rope caught and snagged on the iron hard wood. The boat banged violently against it and then, with no more warning of its going than of its coming, the darkness lifted and an invisible hand smoothed the waters out again.

She clung to the side of the boat, her breath ragged, hearing the last echo of that terrible sucking sound, shaking the water out of her eyes, raising her head to stare into the swollen contorted features of the man whose body had been weighted down and lashed to the fossil trunk and who, with the lowering of the water level, rose up out of the dark loch to peer sightlessly into her face.

TEN

✠ ✠ ✠

The water was still retreating but more slowly, sucked into some underground channel to leave the "stepping stones" free for anyone crazy enough to try to reach the further shore that way.

"And I," said Sister Joan through chattering teeth, "am just about crazy enough."

She wriggled back into the tilting boat and tore her horrified eyes from that dreadful countenance. She could scramble out of the craft and reach the island easily enough, but whom would she tell about her discovery? What guarantee did she have that by the time the authorities had been alerted the body wouldn't have been moved again? Common sense dictated that she try to reach the further shore, but common sense warned her that the freak tide might as suddenly change and she be pulled under the returning waters.

With the remaining oar she pushed herself and the boat free of the tree trunk against which it was jammed and began, slowly and painfully, to scull herself along, hearing the bottom of the boat scrape along the deeply shelving bed of the loch. With intense relief she looked down and glimpsed shale as the gloom lifted and the rushing sound in her ears warned her that the tide was on the turn again. She stepped over the side of the boat, catching her breath as the icy water swirled about her knees and, holding fast the last fossilized trunk, made her way painfully into the shallowest water. The boat, lifted by the incoming water, spun and danced away as if it had been made from matchsticks. She was knocked off her feet by a sudden swell of water and landed on hands and knees, spitting water, on a sandbank.

At least she was safe from drowning. She was also dripping wet and icy cold, the palms of her hands chafed and scratched where she had clung to the side of the boat. She sneezed violently and pulled herself upright, her feet slithering on pebble-strewn sand as she struggled up on to the shore. Behind her there was a rushing noise that filled the world as the tide turned, not gently and gradually as it usually does but with a violence that seemed to her to be almost personal. She had reached the pines and turned to look back at the loch. The tops of the fossilized trees were sinking rapidly from view; the body would have sunk with them, she supposed. There was no sign of the boat.

She would have to get help which meant walking to the village. Turning, she forced her cramped and soaking limbs to carry her forward. The storm was fading, the thunder growling at rarer intervals, only an occasional fork of lightning splitting the sky.

If it starts to rain now, she thought, desperately trying to find some humour in the situation, then I'll start imagining God has a bone to pick with me.

With the thought there came a shower of tingling drops as the heavens opened and threw down the rain.

"I didn't realize," Sister Joan said aloud, squinting up at the sky, "that You were listening."

Not only listening but obviously pushing her into doing something about the body she had found. It was no longer possible to turn her back and assure herself that she had imagined it or that what had happened six years before had nothing to do with her.

Normally there might have been someone out on the loch or on the shore to catch sight of her and run to offer help—she was quite sure that help would have been forthcoming, but the storm had driven everybody within doors, and as she turned into the gully between the high, jagged walls of rock she felt small and alone.

She had reached the bridge when she heard a shout and saw Rory McKensie leaping up the steps at the end of it.

"What the devil happened to you, Sister?" he demanded as he reached her. "I saw you coming on to the bridge and looking half drowned. Have you had an accident?"

"I'll be fine as soon as I've dried out a bit," she assured him. "What are you doing out yourself?"

"Coming over to the retreat to see if you were OK," Rory said.

"That was nice of you," she said in appreciation and sneezed again.

"Come on back up to the house," he urged. "Mum will lend you a dressing-gown or something while your things get dry. You'll catch pneumonia else."

"Do you have a telephone?"

"Yes, in the shop. Why?"

"I need to make a call." She broke off abruptly, remembering that the body weighted down below the water was probably the remains of his father.

"Oh?" Rory gave her a curious glance but made no further comment as he hurried her down the steps and across the road to the village. The street was deserted, the cobbles streaming with rain, and in several of the houses lights burned to combat the gloom.

"I must telephone first," Sister Joan said. "It's important."

"The phone's at the back of the counter. Mum decided to close up early," Rory said. "Look, you give a shout when you've finished and you can come up the stairs."

He bent to push open the shop door. Crime was obviously so rare here that it was unnecessary to lock up everything every hour of the day.

"I'll get Mum to run a hot bath," he said and vanished into the side corridor.

The telephone was an outmoded model, on the wall behind the counter. Sister Joan lifted the counter flap and went through, steeling herself before she lifted the receiver and dialled the emergency number.

"A body?" The disembodied voice sounded faintly disapproving. "In Loch Morag? Are you sure?"

"Perfectly sure." Impatience crisped her voice. "By the line of fossilized trees, weighted down, I think. The freak tide revealed it; the waters have risen again but I am sure the body will still be there. I'm speaking from the McKensie General Store in the village."

"And you say you're a nun?" The voice still sounded bemused.

"Sister Joan from the Order of the Daughters of Compassion. I can give you all those details when someone comes over, but the important thing now is surely to recover the body."

"We'll be out there in about twenty minutes," the voice said.

Putting the receiver back she leaned on the counter for a moment, overcome by weariness and a trembling that came from strain. Then she straightened up and went through to the corridor from which the stairs rose up to the flat over the shop. She had opened her mouth to call when Dolly McKensie appeared at the head of the stairs.

"Come up, Sister," she invited. "I've a hot bath waiting for you and dry clothes while your own are drying out. No sense in catching your death up in that cave."

"You're very kind." Sister Joan climbed the stairs, her sodden habit clinging unpleasantly to her legs.

"Good God, Sister, what happened?" Dolly exclaimed as she stepped into the light.

"I fell into the loch," she answered tiredly. "There's a—a body there, I'm afraid. I just rang the police so they'll be on their way."

For a moment she feared that Dolly was about to overwhelm her with questions, but the other woman thrust at a door on the right, saying brusquely, "The water's nice and hot and I've put some things for you to wear over the rack. If you'd like to pass out your own things I'll put them in the spin dryer, and then give them a good pressing with a hot iron. Rory's making a hot toddy to get the chill out of your bones."

Sister Joan went into the small, steamy bathroom and decided that part of the celestial kingdom must consist of a hot bath into which fragrant bath salts had already been poured. Left to herself she wouldn't have dreamed of using them, but it would have been wicked waste to empty the water out now. Happily conscious that for once duty held hands with inclination she hastily stripped off her garments, passed them obediently around the edge of the door and stepped in with alacrity.

Fifteen minutes later with her body comfortably clad in a loose dark dress under a navy-blue dressing-gown, and her cropped black hair concealed by a paisley patterned scarf, she pushed her feet into a pair of mules

that were a size too big and shuffled out into the landing.

"Come and sit by the fire," Dolly invited. "You need
a hot toddy and some cinnamon toast and don't try to
argue."

"I wasn't dreaming of it," Sister Joan said meekly,
sinking into one of the overstuffed armchairs and accepting the steaming beverage. "I feel awful having to
impose upon you like this but it was an emergency."

"It'll be an hour or two before your own clothes are
ready," Dolly said, seeming by the haste with which she
broke in to be pushing away the offer of any unwel-
come knowledge. "Rory's stuffing your shoes with
newspaper and giving them a good clean."

"The police—"

"Will be here soon enough. They'll likely go down to
the loch first to check your story. What were you doing
to be falling in anyway?"

"I had been visiting at the manse and Morag Sinclair
lent me their boat so that I could row myself back
across the loch."

"Couldn't she drive you back?" Dolly asked sharply.

"She was in a hurry to pick up some books for her
father and then she was going to join him in Aberdeen.
Mrs. McKensie, I think you ought to prepare yourself."

"For the body's being Alasdair?" Dolly spoke quite
calmly, seating herself in an opposite chair.

"I—think so, but of course I can't possibly be sure."

"Oh, it'll be him all right," Dolly said, with an odd
little series of nods as if she had just concluded an ar-
gument with herself. "Nobody else had gone missing in
this area for as long as I can recall. It'll be a relief to
get it identified, save my having to go to the courts to
presume death. I'll get my pension without any bother
I shouldn't wonder."

Sister Joan sipped her scalding drink, glad of the excuse to avert her gaze. She had expected disbelief, an explosion of anger, but not this strange, glinting satisfaction.

"I was afraid you were going to say it was a woman's body or something," Dolly said. "I suppose you could tell? It is six years."

To Sister Joan's relief the bell at the bottom of the stairs rang and the sound of Rory's footsteps, of voices below, held both women motionless.

"Inspector Mackintosh, Mum," Rory said, coming in.

At his heels a burly man in a dark raincoat and slouch hat who looked as if he were about to launch into an impersonation of Humphrey Bogart entered, pulling off the hat to reveal a head of wiry greying hair topping a broad, genial face.

"Mrs. McKensie, we've met before of course." His voice had the softness of the Orkneys. "And this will be Sister Joan?"

"Yes."

"You found the body, Sister Joan?" He sat down on one of the dining chairs and a thin, pale constable who had drifted in like a wraith took another one and opened a notebook with an air of complete boredom.

"Yes."

"Hadn't you better be looking for it?" Dolly said. "It'll be Alasdair—no doubt of it."

"We've a team down at the lochside now," Inspector Mackintosh said. "A few questions, if you'll be so kind, Sister? You're from the Order of the Daughters of Compassion, you say? I've heard of Carmelites and Franciscans."

"Ours is a comparatively small and young order," she explained. "The mother house is in London but we have convents elsewhere—my own is in Cornwall. The order

has a—a retreat up here where sisters can come to renew their spiritual lives if their superiors think it advis-
able."

"And you renew your spirituality by falling into the
loch, do you?" he enquired mildly.

"I had visited the manse," Sister Joan said, refusing
to recognize the gentle sarcasm. "Miss Sinclair was
kind enough to offer me the use of the boat so that I
could row myself back to this side of the loch. The
storm broke without warning—there was a freak tide."

"Peculiar to this loch if I remember rightly. Go on."

"I had drifted close to the old trees and the boat
jammed against them. The body rose up out of the water, head and shoulders, upright. I assume the feet were
weighted, but then it would have been right down on
the bottom, surely?"

"It was clothed?"

She nodded.

"Then it's likely the clothes caught on that old wood
and held the body near the surface," he said. "You did
say 'body,' not 'skeleton'?"

"Body," she said briefly.

"Then it can't have been in the water long. Excuse
me, ladies." He rose and went out again, treading pon-
derously down the stairs. The pale constable remained
where he was, looking wistfully at his notebook.

"You think it's Dad, don't you?" Rory said, breaking
suddenly into the silence.

"Who else?" his mother said with a little flutter of
belligerence.

"Mum, Dad went off six years back," Rory said.
"He'd be a skeleton by now. And the loch was dragged
at the time. They'd have found something then."

"It has to be Alasdair," Dolly said. "Who else could
it be?"

"Still incorrupt? Mum, that's for saints," Rory said in a disgusted tone. "And not all of them either—and Dad was no saint."

The inspector was returning.

"There was a body there," he said. "Hard to tell exactly who it is—the face is somewhat—disfigured, banged against the fossilized trees and so on. We'll get it over to the mortuary and have the whole thing cleared up as best we can. There may be a question of identification."

"I can do that," Rory said quickly. "No need to trouble my mother."

"I was his wife," Dolly said and gave the inspector a hard look. "I'll do any identifying that has to be done. When do you want me over there? I've no car."

"Later this afternoon. I'll send a car," he assured her. "Now, you and I met before, Mrs. McKensie, when we undertook the initial investigation into the disappearance of your husband. I take it that you've heard nothing further since that might be pertinent."

Dolly McKensie frowned slightly as if she were considering and then shook her head. "Nothing to speak of," she said at last.

At least she wasn't going to repeat her belief that her husband had been seeing Catherine Sinclair before running off with someone else, Sister Joan thought.

"In that case I'll be back with a car in about an hour." Inspector Mackintosh glanced at Sister Joan. "There was no sign of any boat, by the way."

"It was probably broken up against the trees and sank. I shall have to explain the matter to Mr. Sinclair," Sister Joan said.

"How did you manage to get ashore? The undertow's pretty fierce."

"I don't know exactly," she admitted. "I stayed in the

boat for as long as I could. I'd lost one oar but I managed to scull myself along with the other one. Then the tide flowed in again and I landed in the shallows—hence the clothes. My own were soaked through."

"The body was near the island, very near," the inspector said. "You didn't think of going there?"

"I believe they have no telephone, Inspector."

Whether or not he considered her answer evasive couldn't be told from the calm impassivity of his face.

"The rain's still pretty bad," he said after a moment. "I can give you a lift back to your—retreat, d'ye call it?"

"Her clothes aren't ready," Dolly said.

"Then I'll call back in about half an hour, shall I? I'll go down and take another look at the loch. Be nice when the rain stops. There'll be a haar later."

He put on his shovel hat and went out again. This time the constable went with him.

"Silly buggers," Dolly said without heat. "Of course it's Alasdair."

"I reckon so," Rory said, and shook his head slightly.

"I am very sorry." Sister Joan spoke quietly.

"Not your fault, Sister. You didn't put the body in the loch," Dolly began, and stopped, frowning. "Put in the loch," she repeated slowly. "Weighted down at the feet? That means he didn't run off at all, doesn't it? Means he was killed."

"Mum, they dragged the loch as far as they could six years back," Rory reminded her.

"Then someone kept him somewhere all that time." Dolly's face twisted into a grimace of disgust.

"I don't think it helps to speculate," Sister Joan said gently. "Look, I'll give my clothes a hot pressing myself, if you don't mind. I'd prefer to have something to do while I'm waiting for the inspector to come back."

"I'll show you the kitchen," Rory said, with a worried glance at his mother. The kitchen was small but spotless, ironing board set up and her garments hung neatly on a rail. Her underwear was dry, she found with relief; the habit and veil only very slightly damp to the touch.

"Your coat will take a few days to dry out," Rory said. "If you leave it here I can lend you an oilskin and sou'wester for the time being. Sister, do you have any idea who might have killed him?"

He had lowered his voice, pushing the door to with the tip of his foot.

"We don't know for certain who the man is yet," Sister Joan said. "We don't know how he died. I think it's best not to make wild guesses."

"I daresay you're right." Rory gave her a disappointed look and went out.

Ten minutes later, clad in her own clothes save for the voluminous oilskin coat and floppy sou'wester that Rory had taken from a cupboard on the landing, Sister Joan hung up the clothes she had briefly borrowed and went back into the living-room.

Dolly McKensie was still seated in the armchair, her head resting on her hand, but the eyes she raised were hard and determined.

"You can save your sympathy, Sister," she said, before the other had time to speak. "I'm sure it's Alasdair, and if it is then it'll save me a deal of expense and trouble. I'm not going to be a hypocrite and pretend to a grief I don't feel. The truth is that he was away more often than he was here when he was alive, and any grief I ever felt was over long before he ran out on me."

Sister Joan was saved from making any further reply by the ringing of the doorbell. A moment later Inspector Mackintosh's official tread sounded on the stair.

"Thank you again for your kindness," Sister Joan said again, and followed him down the stairs.

Outside the rain still teemed and she was conscious of a twitched back curtain at the window of a neighbouring house as she got into the police car.

"Clannish place," Inspector Mackintosh said, to nobody in particular. "You found much difficulty here?"

"People have been very kind," Sister Joan said.

"Old prejudices die hard." He sounded disapproving. "They're behind the times at Loch Morag. All this business must be a bit out of your usual experience."

It was not a question. She was grateful for that because it saved her from the necessity of having to admit that she had been involved, albeit innocently, in other criminal proceedings.* Fortunately her name had been kept out of it all.

The car crossed the road and took a by-pass which avoided the footbridge and brought them into the gully. As they reached the shore she could see through the rain figures moving about near the water-line.

"Odd business," the inspector said. "Where's this retreat of yours then?"

"Up there. There are steps at the steepest part."

"You'll not mind if I come up with you? Pity if you slipped on the wet stone."

"I'm perfectly capable of negotiating a flight of steps," she said crisply.

"Even so." He got out of the car, holding the door open for her. "Just to relieve my mind. It isn't against your rules or anything?"

Sister Joan reflected that the likelihood of a police officer joining a sister up in the retreat was so remote that

*See *Vow of Silence* and *Vow of Chastity*.

it was doubtful any rule had been formulated to deal with it.

"Provided you don't fall down yourself, Inspector," she said sweetly, and began the climb up between the dripping pine trees to where the steps began.

When they reached the top where the step widened into a narrow platform he let out his breath in a long whistle.

"In training for the Olympics, are you?" he enquired.

"It isn't really suitable for elderly members of the order," she admitted.

"And in this weather it isn't suitable for anybody," he said. "You'd better have a word with that mother superior of yours. Tell her to find somewhere a mite less hazardous."

Sister Joan, heroically refraining from pointing out that one didn't "tell" one's prioress anything in the sense he obviously meant it, murmured something and stood within the arch of the rock to take off her oilskins. Her sideways glance at her companion's heavy-duty mackintosh was eloquent.

"You'll not want water dripping all over your cave," the latter said, and unfastened it.

"I can hang the wet garments at the very back of the cave," she said. "I think there's a sort of trough there."

"Cold as charity here," the inspector observed, moving into the cave and scowling around.

"I can offer you a mug of hot tea. There's a primus stove."

"Thanks. All right if I sit here?" He indicated the flat-topped rock that served as stool.

"You may sit on the bed," Sister Joan said, suddenly wanting to giggle. Seldom had she seen a man so far out of his element.

"Very kind of you, Sister." Perching on the extreme

edge he said, watching her busy herself at the stove, "One day you must explain to me why on earth a good-looking woman chooses to go through all this kind of thing. It's beyond my comprehension."

"It's beyond mine sometimes too," she admitted. "You didn't climb all the way up here to ask me about the religious life, did you?"

"I wanted to know if you had anything further to tell me," he said.

She was thankful that dealing with teabags and boiling water made it impossible to look him straight in the eye.

As a law-abiding citizen it was her duty to inform him that she had seen the same body on a previous occasion, that it had then been clad in a monk's habit, that she was certain she had been watched and followed during her visits to the island. There was also, she reminded herself, a higher duty—a loyalty to those who had shown her hospitality, allowed her to penetrate as far as any woman could into the celibacy of the enclosed monastic order. To focus attention on the community too quickly would be damaging to their reputation in an already hostile area. The majority of the villagers would be only too pleased to learn that the police were swarming all over the island.

"What questions would you like to ask me, Inspector?" She handed him the mug and sat down herself on the rock, feeling the residual warmth from the stove and the comfortable dryness of her garments.

"You're here for a—spiritual retreat? For how long?"

"About a month. I can't remain for longer but if the weather becomes very bad then I can use my judgement and leave earlier."

"You live in the Cornwall convent?"

"Yes, but I was trained and professed at the London

house. That's my own special mother house. The main
mother house, the original foundation, is in Holland
since our foundress was Dutch."

She broke off to sip her tea, uneasily aware that she
was talking too fast and too volubly—sure sign of
someone with something to hide.

"If you can just run through what happened earlier
today?" he prompted.

"I decided to take a good long walk round the loch.
I got as far as the manse. The minister, Mr. Sinclair,
was kind enough to entertain me to dinner."

"Are you going?"

"No, I mean that I'd already been to dinner there
with him and his daughter. I called in at the manse and
Morag Sinclair kindly gave me brunch. Her father had
gone to a meeting in Aberdeen, travelling by train, and
she was driving over to meet him and do some shopping before they travelled back together. She was in a
bit of a hurry so I didn't stay too long; anyway she
hadn't time to drive me back but she offered to let me
use the Sinclair boat."

"You can row then?"

"And ride a bicycle and a horse and drive a car. I
wasn't born with a habit and veil on, you know."

"Of course not." He made an apologetic gesture.
"Weren't you a bit nervous of the weather?"

"The storm hadn't even begun," she said. "It started
so rapidly; it was apocalyptic, scaring—I lost one oar,
then I heard the sucking sound as the freak tide took all
the waters away—the old trees rose up out of the water;
I had some idea of reaching them and scrambling on to
the island; then I saw the head and shoulders rising up;
I only thought of getting to a telephone and I sculled
the boat the other way. The water was so shallow that
I was scraping bottom and then I fell out, scrambled

out—I can't remember clearly, and then I got on to the shore and made for the village."

"To the McKensie store?"

"I had that in mind, yes. Mrs. McKensie and her son had been very hospitable to me as well. However I met Rory McKensie on his way over to check that I was all right."

"I'm glad the boy is looking out for you," Inspector Mackintosh said.

"He is a nice person when you get past the prickles. Anyway he went with me back to the shop and I phoned the emergency service from there. Then I dried out—"

"And Mrs. McKensie insisted the body must be that of her husband?"

"It seemed logical," Sister Joan said cautiously.

"I was on the case when Dolly McKensie reported her husband missing six years ago," the inspector said musingly. "She came in about a week after he was due home and said she thought something had happened to him. He was a travelling salesman—toiletries and leather goods—so he was often away, and she didn't start to worry about him for several days—if worry is the right word. She struck me as a woman who'd made her own life—the village store and her son, Rory—and wouldn't have been heartbroken if her husband had never turned up again. We policemen get an instinct about these sorts of things. Anyway we never turned up very much. He'd given up his current job a couple of weeks before and abandoned his car. They'd had a joint bank account from which each could draw at any time. He'd left plenty in it, but he'd drawn an unspecified amount from his personal savings. The bank was coy about telling us exactly how much. We could've obtained a warrant but since there was no question of fraud or foul play then we didn't pursue the matter. The file was kept open in a theoretical sense, but it was fairly clear that he'd done just what his wife suspected and decamped with one of his lady friends."

"More than one?"

"Nobody came forward to help with enquiries, but we reckoned he'd probably had several—er fleeting relationships and finally gone off with someone who really took his fancy. A bit cowardly of him not to put his wife's mind at ease, but from everything we could gather he never showed her much affection, and she's a bit of a tartar from all accounts. Possessive about the boy."

"Human nature is often difficult to fathom."

"Meaning that it is against the rules to gossip?" Inspector Mackintosh gave her an amused glance.

"Meaning I think it's a bit unwise to speculate too wildly without any proof," Sister Joan said.

"That's generally true, but you'd be surprised how often a bit of intelligent speculation eventually turns out to be true," he said, acknowledging the implied rebuke with a faint smile. "However it looks as if we were wrong here. If that body turns out to be Alasdair McKensie then he obviously didn't run off with a lady friend. It was murder—whoever the corpse turns out to be."

"Another speculation?" she asked.

"Your original idea was correct," he said. "His sweater had caught on some projections of the fossilized trees, but his feet were weighted with pieces of iron. They held him upright. And he hadn't been in the water very long. The wool of the sweater would have rotted pretty fast and he'd have sunk to the bottom, even if the body hadn't been in a remarkable state of preservation. The face was damaged, banged against the tree by the force of the wind and waves—but you don't want to hear the gory details."

"No I don't," Sister Joan said firmly.

"Once we get a line on what actually caused his death then we can start looking for the person responsible," he said.

"And the identification."

"We'll have to ask Dolly McKensie to co-operate there. I'm sending a car up for her later this evening. She'll be relieved to qualify for her widow's pension if it proves to be Alasdair McKensie."

"And then he'll be finally laid to rest?"

"I forgot, he was a Catholic, wasn't he? Nominally anyway. What usually happens in a case like that?"

"Any baptized Catholic is entitled to a Catholic funeral," Sister Joan said. "It's assumed that he may well have regained the faith at the last moment."

"Between the saddle and the ground, eh?"

"Something like that. Would you like another cup of tea?"

"Meaning it's time I was going? I think we've covered about everything. With any luck we might get this unpleasant business over without having to disturb the monks on the island."

"The monks?" She was glad that he had risen, turning his back to peer through the aperture where once they had kept a look-out for marauding Vikings.

"He was caught up on the trees nearest to the wharf on the island. It is possible that someone from the island put him in the water—not very probable, but one can't ignore any avenue."

"I suppose not." She bit her lip, torn between her desire to remain silent, her conviction that sooner or later she would have to speak out.

"I'd better be off." The inspector had turned giving

her the kind of long, searching look that made her feel as if she'd murdered the man herself. "I'll get my own coat. You'll be all right here?"

"Yes, of course. If you need anything—"

"I expect to be in touch, but I'll try not to interrupt your retreat too much."

"Thank you." She sat motionless while he ducked into the back of the cave, retrieved his wet coat, and stepped towards the door.

"Inspector, I'm going over to the island tomorrow morning," she said, rising on impulse and going to the door with him. "I have leave to do some painting there, so if you like I could inform the abbot that a body has been found—they may be wondering about the unusual amount of activity on the shore. That would obviate the need for police—lay people to go into the enclosure. I'm sure that Father Abbot will give you any assistance you might want."

"That's very obliging of you, Sister." He had pulled on his coat and now gave her an approving nod. "I doubt if we'll be required to trouble the monks. You don't go in for murdering lapsed Catholics, I take it?"

That was meant as a joke, she supposed, shaking her head and smiling politely.

"Take care then, Sister," he said cheerfully, and went cautiously down the steps into the rain.

And now I have landed myself with more responsibility, Sister Joan thought, staring into the blurred shapes of the pine trees below. And if this whole matter isn't cleared up very fast I'll be forced to tell the police all about what happened to me in the crypt.

Sighing, she went back into the silence of the cave.

ELEVEN

✠ ✠ ✠

By morning the rain had become a fine white mist that lay like snow over the waters of the loch. The rain itself had ceased and a faint amber sun showed fitfully between the still louring clouds. She had slept deeply without dreaming, which proved, she thought ironically, that sound slumber wasn't always a sign of an easy conscience. It had been her duty to inform Inspector Mackintosh about the body in the monk's habit and modern shoes; she ought to have reported it even after the body had disappeared; she certainly ought to have told him the whole story yesterday. To seek to protect the privacy of a religious community didn't give her the right to bend the law of the land. It was an offence to withhold information from the authorities. Yet she had slept as sweetly as a baby.

She was hungry, having neglected to eat more than a couple of apples before beginning her evening meditations. She found some bread and fried it with a couple of tomatoes—not breakfast as ordered by the rule but extremely satisfying to the stomach.

She scraped the plate, treated herself to a second cup of tea with the inward proviso that if one was going to break a rule one may as well break it thoroughly, and put on the oilskins. The fear that Brother Cuthbert might not be around—she had, after all, told him not to inconvenience himself when the weather was bad, was dissipated when, having reached the bottom of the steep climb with no more than a momentary slip, she saw his dark figure standing on the shore in the usual place.

"I wasn't sure if you'd be coming, Sister," he greeted her. "That was a bad storm yesterday. We were all in our cells while it was raging, praying for those in peril on the sea."

"Or the loch," she said.

"There wouldn't have been any fishermen out there. I came to the wharf to check the boat hadn't been blown adrift later on, and there were some people on the other shore—this side, I mean. It was too rainy to tell who they were, and in any case I'm always having to confess to idle curiosity," he said. "It isn't that I mean to be inquisitive but the world's so full of interesting things. The people in it constantly astonish me— Father Abbot says I ought to have taken the name of Brother Wonderland, except that there's no such saint."

"Why Cuthbert?" She accepted his help into the boat.

"We can choose our own," he said. "I used to do a lot of hiking and hill-walking—"

"If it's private . . .?" she said, noting a hesitation.

"It sounds a bit pompous, that's all," Brother Cuthbert said. "I mean that I always seemed to be looking for something, hunting like Saint Cuthbert—and then I came to Loch Morag and I found out that I'd been looking for myself, for the life that would let me be more myself—I'm not explaining this very well."

"I think you've explained it beautifully," Sister Joan said softly. "I know exactly what you mean. And I'm sure that your prayers must have helped someone in peril."

"Hey, wouldn't that be something, Sister!" he exclaimed, a broad grin of delight transforming him into a schoolboy dressed up as a monk. "Are you going to paint today? It's pretty wet outside still."

"I was hoping to meet with Father Abbot, if he can spare me half an hour," she said.

"I can make enquiries for you, Sister. I don't think he has any pressing business this morning. Did you know there was a freak tide yesterday? The old trees were above the waterline for a few minutes—"

"You saw them?" Her tone was suddenly sharp.

"No, I was in my cell, but I heard one of the other brothers mention the fact. I think the freak tides used to occur more frequently and last for much longer in the old times, else they'd never have used the polled trees as stepping stones. Watch yourself on the wharf, Sister. I'm thinking of sprinkling gravel to make it less slippery. Some of the people who come over for mass aren't so young."

She climbed up on to the wharf and waited for him to tie up the boat. Her mind was working rapidly along unpleasant lines. Whoever had seen the waters go down during the freak tide must have seen her struggling towards the further shore, must have known that for a few minutes, at least, she had been in real danger.

Whoever had been near enough to see the waters sucked away must have left his cell and come down to the shore. Because he feared there might be a freak tide that would uncover what was hidden? If so then that same person must have realized that she too had seen it. She wondered why he had not removed the body but it had probably been too risky at that particular time when, at any moment, one of the other brothers might have emerged from his cell to take a look at the weather.

"Sister?" Brother Cuthbert was looking at her enquiringly.

"I'm sorry. What did you say?"

"If you wait in the scriptorium I'll find out if Father Abbot is free."

"Yes. Thank you."

The oilskins flapping around her ankles she walked on to the large building. It was bitterly cold in the scriptorium. She went over to her easel and lifted the cloth, heaving a sigh of relief as she saw that the damp atmosphere hadn't caused any damage. The picture was good, she decided, without vanity. Someone greater than herself had guided her brush.

She propped the painting against the wall and took out her sketch pad. For the "Winter" version she would sketch the same scene and paint from her own imagination the way it would look when snow iced the ground and the trees were edged with the hard, brilliant light of December.

She had made a fair start on the preliminary study when the outer door swung open and Brother Cuthbert's red head appeared.

"I'm to take you to Father Abbot now, Sister," he said.

That meant the parlour with its chilly anteroom. She wiped charcoal from her fingers and put on her sou'wester which she'd taken off. The bright yellow oilskin was so much brighter than her usual garb that she could only hope it wasn't going to shock any of the community who had seen it.

"Oh, I found the plastic," Brother Cuthbert said cheerfully as they left the scriptorium.

"Plastic? Oh, yes, the plastic."

She had forgotten about the large sheet of heavy plastic used for covering those who died within the community.

"It was folded up in my place in chapel. It must have blown away after all."

"Who found it?" she asked.

"I don't know, Sister. It was careless of me to lose it in the first place and whoever found it obviously put it in my place as a gentle reminder. You know how it is."

Yes, she knew very well the numerous ways in which one could break a rule without even realizing it. Spilling tea, neglecting to finish up the crumbs from one's plate, letting a soup pan boil over and thus causing wastage—all faults of carelessness and inattention which were not important in the secular world but were important in the religious life which had to be lived at a high degree of attention.

They were in the anteroom again. She glanced involuntarily up at the spyhole high in the wall but no shadow moved behind it. Brother Cuthbert gave her a cheerful grin and flapped out again.

"Sister Joan, good morning. Please come in." The tall abbot stood aside from the door he had just opened to allow her to pass into the parlour. This morning no fire burned in the grate but there was a jug of coffee on the table.

"Good morning, Father Abbot." She entered the parlour, took the chair he indicated, and meekly accepted the mug of coffee he handed her.

"It's a cold morning, Sister," he said conversationally. "Winter is just around the corner I fear. Won't you take off your er—hat?"

"I beg your pardon."

She hastily removed the sou'wester and smoothed down her veil.

"A new fashion for nuns?" He gave her a benignly teasing look. "I am, of course, out of touch with modern customs."

"No indeed, Father Abbot. My own outer garments got very wet and I was obliged to borrow this," she assured him. "I don't usually walk round looking like a daffodil on legs."

The abbot chuckled, taking a chair by the table and regarding her steadily. The polite preliminaries were over and his tone became businesslike.

"You wanted to see me, Sister?"

"Yes, Father Abbot." She put down the mug, folded her hands tightly together, and said, "I'm afraid the police are making enquiries locally. During the freak tide yesterday a body was revealed in the loch, caught by its clothing on the fossil trees. I was rowing across the loch at the time, having borrowed the Sinclair boat, and I came to face to face with it."

"What a dreadful experience, my dear Sister!" His fine boned, aristocratic old face expressed distress. "But how unwise of you to be on the loch in the first place."

"The storm blew up without warning," she reminded him. "Fortunately I did manage to reach the shore and make my way to the village to telephone the police. They came over and retrieved the body."

"Brother Cuthbert mentioned at recreation that there was an unusual amount of activity on the opposite shore," he said. "I'm afraid I chided him for being over-inquisitive. Brother Cuthbert is still very young and not yet tuned completely into the inner life. The incident must have been most distressing."

"The point is," said Sister Joan, "that the body was weighted at the feet so that it stood upright in the water."

"A suicide?" The finely shaped hand traced a cross. "That really is distressing. Suicide is such an unnecessary act. Nine times out of ten a problem can be solved with counselling and courage."

"The police don't think it was suicide," Sister Joan said. "I think it would be very difficult for anyone to weight themselves down and then jump in. They would have had to wade into the deep water with their ankles bound."

She had no idea whether or not the ankles had been actually bound, but her impulsive attempt to catch the abbot out bore no fruit.

"But this is very serious," he said gravely. "You are suggesting that foul play was involved."

"It seems so."

"The world is in a very sad state," he observed.

"There is a possibility that the body may be that of Alasdair McKensie."

"The man who disappeared?" The gravity increased. "This will be a sad blow to his wife, I suppose—or will there be also a measure of relief? I think the stress of not knowing what has happened to someone must be almost as bad, perhaps worse, than knowing the missing person is dead. Thank God I have no personal experience of such anguish. Is the identification certain?"

"I don't know yet," Sister Joan said.

"Alasdair McKensie was a Catholic, was he not? He did not, I understand, practise his faith and as we are enclosed here there was nothing I could do to influence the matter. Indeed I never even met him. Was it a question of the funeral?"

"He has the right to a Catholic one, but I imagine there will be a priest available—possibly from Aberdeen?"

"Yes indeed, but we, as a community, will, of course, pray. You must try not to dwell upon it too much, Sister."

"The inspector may have to question the community," Sister Joan said.

"Question us?" The abbot reared up his head like a handsome old warhorse who hears the echoes of a bugle. "I fail to see how we can possibly be of help."

Sister Joan hesitated, her hands tightly clenched. She could speak out, tell the abbot about her visit to the crypt and the discovery of the body in the modern shoes, but to tell him something she hadn't yet reported to the police was surely irresponsible.

"It's possible that a member of the community has seen something," she said cautiously. "Somebody weighted the body and put it into the water, near enough to the fossilized trees for the clothing to snag on it—someone might have seen and not realized what he was seeing."

"My dear Sister Joan, if one of us had seen a body being slipped into the loch, I am sure the action couldn't have been mistaken for anything more innocent."

"Perhaps someone borrowed your boat?"

"Loch Morag is plentifully supplied with fishing boats. There would be no need for someone to come over to the island to borrow ours," he protested. "And how would this mythical person get back to the mainland? The spur that joins us to the north shore is blocked by rubble and barbed wire and a very deep ditch that is flooded for much of the year."

"And your boat has never been missing? Never been found on the opposite shore?"

"No, of course not. Sister, if the police have any ideas that this very sad discovery has anything whatsoever to do with the community they are entirely on the wrong track," he said impatiently. "Even weighted the body must surely have shifted position quite markedly during the last six years."

Sister Joan took up her coffee mug again and drained

the cooling liquid. She could, of course, say that there
was every indication that the body had only just been
put into the loch but it was probably wiser to keep silent.

"Inspector Mackintosh, the police officer in charge of
the case, is hoping not to have to trouble the community," she said at last. "I promised him that I would
mention the matter to you in case you could help with
any enquiries."

"I doubt if anyone here would be able to tell you or
the police anything," the abbot said, beginning to rise.
"It was considerate of the inspector to hesitate before
disturbing the peace of the cloister. I will, naturally,
mention the recent occurrence without any of the atten-
dant speculations, in order that the deceased may receive our prayers, but for practical purposes we are
quite useless, I fear."

"And your boat has never been missing?"

"Never, Sister. I can assure you of that quite categor-
ically. If you will excuse me now I must return to my
duties."

"Yes, of course. Thank you, Father Abbot."

She rose politely as he left, his robe creating a cold
draught of air as he strode through the door. That he
was more agitated than he was willing to admit was
clear to her, but the exact source of his disquiet was impossible to pinpoint.

She moved to the table, bare except for the coffee jug
and mugs, and looked through the small casement window into a tiny courtyard where a couple of holly
bushes promised gaiety during the coming winter. There
were some papers lying on the broad sill—notes for a
sermon, she realized, glancing down at them. There was
something familiar about the words but then most sermons were much of a muchness, she supposed. There

was no excuse for her to linger here, and she turned and went out again, not pausing in the antechamber.

The mist was still thick, hanging low over the wall beyond which the separate cells were grouped. It must be an extra discomfort on winter mornings to have to hurry from the cells over to the main buildings where the refectory would be situated. At least they were spared that in her own convent which had been converted from a stately mansion and retained some of its bygone elegance.

When it was discovered that the body had been dead for six years questions would be asked about the extraordinary state of preservation of the body and then someone might remember the crypt—if its existence was generally known. The thought that it might not be threw the responsibility for revealing the fact squarely back on to her own shoulders. She bit her lip in exasperation.

For the moment she might as well get on with her work. She jammed her sou'wester over her head and plodded back to the scriptorium. After her large breakfast she would be able to work right through until evening without stopping.

She took off the oilskins, draped them over a bench, blew on her chilly fingers, and set to work again, sketching and shading the outlines. This would be a night study, she resolved, with snow gleaming under a single star and a mellow light beaming out of the open door of the church.

As usual the joy of creation pushed everything else to the back of her mind. One more session would do it, she decided, and propped the blank canvas on the easel—beginning to transfer the sketch she had completed in broader, more sweeping lines before she mixed her colours.

The chilly atmosphere was forgotten as she worked on. The complete absorption she could find in painting had worried her once. Other people found the same satisfaction in prayer. Mother Agnes, her first prioress, had untangled her feelings in her usual dry, cool manner.

"Sister, prayer and devotion may be expressed in many ways. Provided your subject is worthy and your treatment of it spiritual, then your work becomes a prayer in itself."

Her old boyfriend, Jacob, had held different views. Art should shock and startle, rouse people out of complacency, alter their conceptions of beauty. Yet in the end Jacob had returned to his own faith and she had entered the religious life. She thought of him so seldom that to think of him now gave her a little shock as if she had opened a door into a room she had locked years before.

"Sister Joan, Brother Brendan has sent over a mug of soup and some bread," Brother Cuthbert said, coming in after a brief rat-tat on the door.

"How very kind." She looked in some dismay at the steaming mug and hunk of bread he had put down in a cleared space on the long table. Everybody seemed bent on feeding her up, which meant a definite conflict between rules. Greed was to be avoided and discouraged at all costs; on the other hand one must accept with humble gratitude anything that was offered without having asked for it.

"When two rules seem to conflict then follow the one that causes no hurt to other people," her novice mistress had said.

And jolly sensible too, she decided, picking up the wide mug and dipping a sliver of bread into the spicy vegetable broth.

"I say, Sister, this is absolutely super!" Brother

Cuthbert was regarding the two paintings with youthful enthusiasm.

"Thank you," she said.

"Not that I know anything about painting," he deprecated. "Strumming a lute is the only artistic talent I have, and some musically aware people might be a bit doubtful about that. But why have you made the paintings so lonely?"

"Lonely?" She squinted at them critically.

"No people going in and out of the church," he said. "I'm sorry, Sister—I really don't know anything about the subject. I'd better get on—see you later."

But he was right, she thought, staring at her work. At the heart of it was an emptiness she hadn't noticed before. A church symbolized more than a lovely building set in a beautiful landscape.

"Bother the boy!" she muttered under her breath, removing the new study and replacing it on the easel with the finished painting. "Bother him, but he's absolutely right."

She began swiftly to outline a small figure, dwarfed by the height of the church, looking up at the sky with its cerulean blue and tiny, lamb-white clouds.

The task completed and the soup eaten, she exchanged the paintings again, spent a happy hour on the winter study and laid down her brush at last with a pleased sigh. Her arm ached and the energy that had fuelled her was draining away.

She damped the covering cloth in the little toilet room, put on the oilskin coat and sou'wester again and went out into the mist. It was clammy and vaguely unpleasant; breathing it in was like breathing in water and made her cough.

It had been a good session. She walked towards the church, seeing its outlines take shape through the whiteness. Her footsteps sounded curiously muffled in the silence. When she reached the church door she was surprised to discover that she was trembling slightly. Nerves had no place in the cloister. Another maxim from her old novice mistress came into her head, and she frowned. Her brain seemed to be crammed full of other people's thoughts as if she had lost the ability to think for herself. For the first time in years an old fear was surfacing. Lay people often joked that it was almost impossible to tell one nun from another, an obvious absurdity but one fuelled by the conformity of behaviour to be found in a community. She had learnt that before the individuality could flower the personality must be controlled and tempered. But she rather liked her own personality, she thought with a tiny flash of rebellion. The notion of losing herself so thoroughly in the rule that she became merely a living expression of it gave her the sensation of standing on a shifting sandbank while around her the waters drained away.

She pushed open the door, blessed herself and went up the aisle to kneel at the altar rail. It was time to thank God for the inspiration that had moved her pencil and her brush, time to offer a prayer for guidance, to ask for mercy for the man in the loch and the one who had put him there. It was time, in short, to hand everything over to the Boss and stop imagining she could shape the course of events.

From the dark stalls where the brothers worshipped, hidden from the lay congregation by the wooden barrier, came a sudden rustling noise. Too loud for mice or even a rat. It came again and with it a long-drawn-out sigh, a sound that hung eerily on the silent air. The short hairs at the back of her neck bristled slightly and a light sweat broke out under the edge of her veil.

Someone was watching her. Someone, standing back

in the deepest shadows, was looking over the barrier, watching her as she knelt. If she turned her head she would glimpse . . . ? Had her life depended on it she could not have turned her head towards that shadowed place where someone watched her. She kept her head bent, her hands cradled. If someone wanted to terrify her then they were being extremely successful.

"Hail Mary, full of grace . . ." Her whispered petition steadied her as the words that never changed were breathed out into the air.

The rustling came again, so briefly that it might have been imagined, and then the church door opened and Brother Cuthbert's feet padded down the aisle.

She cast a swift look to her right but the feeling of being watched had gone, and she crossed herself and went to meet Brother Cuthbert with an assumption of calmness that deceived Brother Cuthbert and almost deceived herself.

"I haven't interrupted you?" he asked anxiously.

"Not at all. I was very glad to see you," she said honestly.

"The mist is still pretty thick and it may get worse. Sometimes it hangs about for days in the autumn," he said, genuflecting to the altar. "Father Abbot thinks we'd be wise to cross now."

"Very sensible," she said briskly. "You'll be all right coming back?"

"I'll be fine," he assured her. "The wind's dropped and I know the loch like the back of my hand. Ah, shall we take the plastic? It's still in my stall."

That, she realized, had been the cause of the rustling sound—the heavy plastic rubbed between fingers that were perhaps contemplating the risks involved in covering her with its smothering folds.

"The oilskins are protection enough, Brother. We'd better go."

She was already at the door. Brother Cuthbert cast a wistful glance altarwise and followed her.

The mist was not dispersing but intensifying, its whiteness shrouding them. When they reached the wharf she could barely see the boat moored there.

"Here we are then, Sister." Helping her down he said abruptly, the usual optimistic note dying out of his voice, "Father Abbot tells us that a body's been found in the loch. That must have been very upsetting."

"Since I found it—yes," she said dryly.

"You actually found it? You didn't say."

"I thought it more correct to inform the abbot first."

"Yes, of course. Silly of me. Father Abbot didn't say who had actually found it. He did say there was a chance it might be the remains of someone who disappeared from the village several years ago. It's funny that it's not been found until now."

The abbot had evidently given the brothers an edited version.

"It's probable," she said.

"Before my time," Brother Cuthbert said, plying an oar vigorously. "What a sad way to end—we shall all be praying like mad whoever he was."

"Will you be able to pick me up tomorrow if the mist has cleared?" she asked. "I want to finish the second painting. Only I'd not wish you to catch a cold on my account—your habit doesn't look very dry."

"Oh, a shower of rain or a spoonful of mist never caused me any trouble," he assured her. "Anyway I have a spare habit. A third one."

"A third one?"

"The rule allows us two, worn turn and turn about.

Brother Anthony has just given me another one—tells me it turned up unexpectedly and I'm to keep it."

"Who's Brother Anthony?" she asked sharply.

"He has charge of the linen but he gets a bit muddled these days. Over eighty."

Then it wasn't likely to have been old Brother Anthony who had lugged the dead weight of the body around.

"Brother Cuthbert, have all the brothers got two habits?" she asked.

"Even the abbot. We must all follow the rule. Every fifteen years or so new ones are made and distributed. I've a while to wait. The problem is that I'm not the most careful of people so Brother Anthony reckoned I'd better have a third habit—for best."

"Do any of the brothers have only one habit?" she asked.

"I don't know, Sister. If someone had lost one it would have been reported. It could belong to one of the community who died. We are buried in one habit and the other is handed down to someone else. Is it important?"

"Just idle curiosity. That's my besetting sin," she said evasively.

"If you only have one then you're lucky, Sister." He grinned over his shoulder and plied his oars more energetically.

It was a small miracle that he seemed to know exactly where he was, she thought. All round them was the thick, white, clinging mist. Yet he landed as far as she could tell in exactly the same place as usual, jumping into the shallows to pull the boat up to the shingle.

"Father Abbot says that I'm to come with you to make sure you get up to the retreat safely," he said. "In this mist you might lose your footing."

"It is bad," she agreed.

"What they call round here a bit of a haar. Not a day for hill-walking."

She murmured assent and followed his tall figure as it went ahead into the whiteness. There was something reassuringly protective in his presence. Having recognized that she frowned, wondering why she should feel she needed protection.

"You go first, Sister. If you slip I'll break your fall," he said, pausing at the bottom of the steep, pineclad path.

"And how," she demanded, "are you going to get down?"

"You forget my hobby used to be walking and hill-climbing," he reminded her. "I'm very sure-footed and don't worry about falling on me. I'm strong as an ox."

"Right then." She started the ascent, the pine trunks looming out of the mist as she followed the twisting path. Now and then her feet skidded on wet pine needles but the trunks were close enough to grasp and haul herself back. Nevertheless by the time they had gained the steps she was panting slightly.

"Take a little rest, Sister. At your age it isn't good to overdo things," his anxious voice insisted.

"Very kind of you," she said dryly, resisting an impulse to sprint ahead and disprove his rooted image of her as someone on the edge of senility. There were times when Brother Cuthbert made her feel positively middle-aged.

The steps were wet and slippery. Gripping the rail as she went up them she resolved to send a report to the other convents, detailing the inconveniences of retaining a retreat half way up a cliff in a Scottish loch. As far as she could tell its main advantage lay in the fact that it might prove an excellent means of disposing of an elderly nun who had become a bit of a nuisance in her convent. The irreverent notion made her want to giggle.

"Here we are then!" Brother Cuthbert said from below.

"Will you come in for a hot drink, Brother?" She opened the front door with relief.

"That's very kind of you, Sister, but I have to get back. I just wanted to make sure you were all right— and don't worry about me slipping. I'm sure-footed as a goat. God bless until tomorrow."

The black robed figure turned and in a moment more was swallowed by the swirling mist.

A nice lad if a trifle tactless now and then, she decided, letting herself in and relishing the sensation of having reached a refuge. Perhaps after all the isolation had its charms.

She took off her oilskins and hung them at the back of the cave. Despite the "bit of a haar" the inner walls were dry and when she had lit the stove and made herself a mug of tea the atmosphere became positively homelike.

The rest of the day was her own, to be employed, she told herself severely, in spiritual disciplines. First the record of her faults to be written up, then the mysteries of the rosary to be recited, then a passage from her Prayer Book to be studied and analysed. Her papers and books were piled on the ledge. It was dim in the cave, spirals of white mist trailing through the aperture through which the monks of old had kept a look-out for the Viking ships.

She lit a candle and sat down to sort through the pile and find her book of faults. A piece of paper, torn raggedly along one edge, fluttered to the floor.

*. . . and feel your sweet mouth against mine and the
little fluttering breaths of desire . . .*

The piece of a love letter caught in the tree, the tall
cowled boatman striding into the grove with Morag
Sinclair as the darkness shielded them. The images co-
alesced in her mind into a too vivid picture. That bold,
black handwriting she knew, was seen last in the parlour
with the notes for a sermon written by—it had to be the
abbot since the parlour was his domain and he would
certainly preach numerous sermons. It wasn't the words
that had seemed familiar, but the handwriting.

TWELVE

✠ ✠ ✠

She sat for a long time staring at the paper; her immediate impulse was to tear it across over and over; it was an impulse she resisted, remembering incidents in the past when she had been too apt to rush headlong into action. Her surmise that it had been written by the abbot rested only on the probability of the sermon having been penned by him, of his being the only member of the community who could come and go by boat in secret without the other monks knowing. The abbot, she told herself, must be in his seventies; Morag Sinclair was twenty-three. Was it even remotely likely that a man who had devoted his life to the cloister should in his old age take to writing passionate love letters to a girl old enough to be his granddaughter? Her instincts told her that it wasn't so, that there had to be some other explanation. Her reason whispered that the most unexpected people often did the most unexpected things.

And it had nothing to do with her. Whatever the truth she was not the keeper of the abbot's conscience. The fragment of passionate longing had, as far as she could see, nothing at all to do with the discovery of the body in the loch.

She folded the paper neatly and put it into her suitcase. Before she left the retreat she would be guided somehow as to the right course of action to take.

For the rest of the day she concentrated upon her own shortcomings until her conscience felt as if it had been spring-cleaned. At the rate she was going, she thought wryly, she would soon need a new book of faults.

The mist was beginning to clear. That clinging whiteness that drifted through the aperture like trails of white smoke had dispersed and the grey sky was flaming into an unexpected sunset. She paused to munch an apple and eat the last of the biscuits she had and lit her candle. In a little while she would get down to a good solid chunk of prayer—the sovereign remedy in times of trouble.

Outside there was a noise, so faint that it almost died before it reached her ears. She sat bolt upright on the rock, her heart beating uncomfortably fast. Was it perhaps some animal or other? Her imagination promptly supplied dinosaurs.

Another scraping noise and then a loud rapping on the door. Animals, she told herself firmly, didn't knock on doors. She rose to answer it, seeing as she pulled back the heavy door, the thickset frame of Inspector Mackintosh.

"Am I disturbing you, Sister?" He already had his hat in his hand.

"Not in the least. You're much more welcome than a dinosaur," she said in a flurry, stepping back into the cave.

"Yes, well, I hope that's so." He closed the door behind him and shot her a somewhat puzzled glance.

"Isolation isn't giving me hallucinations," she hastened to explain. "I heard some scraping and my imagination started working overtime. Please sit down."

"The scraping was the sound of my boots." He sat down on the edge of the bed.

"Yes, of course. May I offer you something?"

"Not for me, Sister. A bit more light would be welcome though." He looked round at the shadowed rock walls.

Sister Joan obediently lit two more candles and placed them on the ledge. When she sat down again she saw that the inspector was studying her thoughtfully, his big, greying head tipped slightly to one side.

"I'd not like my daughter to enter a convent," he said abruptly. "Not even if I was a Catholic. It's an unnatural life."

"A supernatural life," she corrected. "A life lifted above the natural order in an attempt to create a living bridge between heaven and earth. Not that we always achieve our ends. Inspector, you didn't climb all the way up here to discuss theology with me, did you?"

"No, Sister, I didn't." He frowned as if he were rearranging his thoughts, then said, "Dolly McKensie identified her husband."

"It was Alasdair McKensie then?" She crossed herself, murmuring a brief prayer for the reposal of souls. "I am sorry but in one way I suppose it must be a relief to her to get confirmation."

"She'll be able to draw her widow's pension without going through the court," he said dryly.

"Yes."

"The pathologist is still continuing with his investigations," he said. "There are some puzzling features about the corpse. It is in an unusually good state of preservation for a body that has been apparently dead for six years. The initial findings which cannot be confirmed bear out the theory that the body was put into the loch quite recently. The damage to the face is recent. The rest of the body is remarkably well preserved, almost as if it had been embalmed though I understand that isn't the case. One does occasionally come across such medical aberrations, of course, but not after long immersion in water. I have a hunch it was hidden on land for a long time."

"I see." She spoke slowly, her eyes raised to his face.

"I've heard reports of a crypt," he said. "A place where the atmosphere is such that bodies are gradually mummified instead of decaying in the usual way. Have you heard of such a crypt, Sister?"

"Yes, I have. I understand that in the old days the abbots of the community were placed in the crypt as a mark of honour."

"Been down in this crypt, Sister?"

"Yes, I have. It is seldom visited these days since all the members of the community are now buried in the enclosure cemetery when they die."

"Have you anything else to tell me, Sister?" His shadow flared, gigantic on the wall.

"Not yet, Inspector." She clenched her hands in her lap to still their trembling.

"I'm not wishful to intrude into the community unless I have good reason," the inspector said. "We don't know yet how he died. On the other hand if the circumstances warrant it then I'll have no hesitation. Is the crypt open to the general public?"

"It isn't locked, but the general public don't wander around on the island," she said. "There is a mass offered on Sundays which the lay congregation attend, but they go to the church and come away again after the service."

"But it would be possible to row over to the island and go into the church?"

"Quite possible," she said promptly. "There are no

bolts and bars save in the enclosed part of the community—they are on the inside, of course, but the church is almost certainly kept unlocked all the time and the crypt isn't locked either."

"A bit risky that in this day and age."

"Not really, Inspector. It would have to be a pretty determined vandal to go to the trouble of rowing across to the island in order to break into a church or a crypt where, as far as I know, nothing valuable is kept."

"As you say, Sister. Most churches have to be locked up now unless there's a service on. It's a sad reflection on modern life."

"As far as I know nothing was ever stolen from the church," she said.

"I was thinking that somebody might have taken something from the crypt," he said. "Taken something that they'd put there in the first place. How does that theory strike you?"

"As a rational one. Inspector, if you want to ask me a direct question—"

"Not until we find out how Alasdair McKensie met his death. It might only be a matter of concealment of a body—a grave matter to be sure but not as bad as— well we'll have to see how it goes, shan't we?"

"Yes." She looked down at her entwined fingers and said diffidently, "I won't withhold any information if it's pertinent but you must understand there are other loyalties too. Men don't enter monasteries because they crave police investigations."

"That's why I'm not rushing over to ask any questions yet," he said. "The local people have always been a mite suspicious of monks—smacks of old-time popery and the like. If we go blundering in we could upset the balance that's been achieved already. However if there has been a crime committed then nobody is above the law."

"That's—considerate of you, Inspector."

"We're not as flat-footed as folk appear to think," he said. "Well, I'd best be off home. My wife'll never believe I've been cliff climbing."

"Hardly a cliff," she demurred.

"Steep enough for me." He had risen, still looking at her with an expression that was almost avuncular. As Sister Joan also rose he said, "I've been making a few enquiries. You're not entirely new to police matters, are you? Played quite a useful role in a couple already."

"Not by my choice," she said, flushing. "Nothing ever got into the papers."

"That's true, but when I rang the station nearest your convent to check up that you really are who you say you are I was informed that you had twice been of some considerable help in that area."

"You checked up on me?" For a moment she was disconcerted. Then her sense of humour bubbled up. "It was good of you not to telephone the convent itself. My prioress would be less than happy to learn that I was mixed up in anything else. I really don't try to make a habit of this."

"I thought it wiser not to bother your prioress. I am conscious that nuns don't usually seek publicity. You were a great help to my Cornish colleagues seemingly."

Though his words were not a question his expression was. Sister Joan spoke cautiously. "That's true. However I do know my duty as a citizen, Inspector. I also reserve the right to make up my mind alone about some things. I hope you understand that."

"I understand but don't entirely approve. For the time being I'll not press you."

"Thank you, Inspector. You'll take care going down the steps? I have a torch if you want to borrow it."

"I have one myself but the mist is clearing and I have twenty-twenty night vision. About the inquest—" He paused on his way to the door.

"I will be there if I'm needed."

"Probably only your statement will be required. If there are any questions—I can ask the Coroner if he has any particular problems and then you can slant your statement to incorporate them."

"That would indeed be kind." She felt a small surge of gratitude. "The order prefers that we don't get ourselves into the newspapers."

"I'll bear it in mind. You won't catch cold here? I'd not like to think of my daughter being stuck in this place."

"She probably hasn't had my training," Sister Joan said. "I appreciate your concern but I'm fine."

"Right then, Sister. Good night to you." He went out, closing the door. There was silence for a moment as he obviously got his bearing and then the soft scraping of a boot against stone.

She sat down again, feeling the silence close round her again. Silence and isolation repeated over and over spelt loneliness. If there had been a telephone in the retreat she would have rung her convent, just for the comfort of hearing a familiar voice. It wasn't any use. Despite her resolve it was impossible to settle down to her devotions. She went to the back of the cave and struggled into the oilskins, found her torch, and put out the candles. Perhaps now wasn't the most tactful time but she had the excuse of collecting her coat and scarf when she called on Dolly McKensie.

A brisk wind was whirling away the last ribbons of mist. Overhead the first stars were venturing. She held the torch steadily and made her way down the steps and the slope that ended in the rough shingle of the loch side. The damp air on her face was refreshing and she quickened her step as she turned into the gully and made for the bridge.

There were lights in the houses along the village street. Families would be gathered together now about their television sets, or discussing the finding of the body in the loch. She wondered if any neighbour had called in to express sympathy with Dolly McKensie over the sad finish to her long waiting, but she doubted it. They might wish to call but from what she had gleaned Dolly McKensie had never made any particular efforts to assimilate herself into the life of the locals. She served them in the store, watched jealously and proudly over her son, and kept herself to herself. She had only talked to Sister Joan because she knew the latter's stay was temporary.

When she rang the bell there was a pause and then a window was opened over her head.

"You've not forgotten your key surely?" a voice questioned fretfully.

"It's Sister Joan. I hope I'm not disturbing you." She tilted back her head to answer and saw the frizzy outline of Dolly's hair framed in the casement.

"I'll open the door from up here. Just give it a push and come up the stairs."

The head withdrew and the window was closed. A faint buzzing announced the freeing of the lock and she pushed the door wider, closed it behind her, and mounted the feebly lit stairs to where the other woman was opening the flat door.

"Nasty night for you to be out, Sister," she commented, leading the way into the comfortable living-room with the overstuffed chairs. On the table was the inevitable pot of tea.

"It isn't too bad at all now," Sister Joan said. "I came to ask if my coat and scarf were dried out and to return the oilskins. It was very good of Rory to lend them."

"Oh, they're not Rory's. Alasdair used to wear them. If I'd had any sense I'd have realized he wasn't coming back and thrown them out ages ago. They were the only things of his that I kept. Would you like a cup of tea, Sister? It's only just brewed."

"Half a cup would be very welcome, thank you. Shall I put these in the bathroom?" She was stripping off the oilskins, feeling a sudden inexplicable unwillingness to go on wearing them.

"I'll put them away. Help yourself to some tea, Sister—your own coat is good and dry now; I'll bring it out to you."

She bustled out and Sister Joan obediently poured herself some tea. The room felt warm and airless and she fought down a desire to fling open the window and stick her head out into the cool evening.

"Here we are, Sister. I'll join you in another one myself." Dolly had returned, Sister Joan's coat and scarf over her arm.

"I heard that you had identified Mr. McKensie," the latter said diffidently.

"Yes, it was him all right even if the face had been battered against those old trees. I guessed that it would be him the minute I heard someone had been found."

"I'm very sorry. I know it's been a long time but to find out for sure must be—"

"He was never much use as a husband when he was around," Dolly said with a little flare of resentment. "Never here when he was here, if you know what I mean."

"Nevertheless, I wondered if you needed any help about funeral arrangements, but I suppose that will be seen to?"

"The priest over in Aberdeen will conduct the service," Dolly said. "He and I hadn't any family to speak of, so it'll be quiet. Have you seen that inspector?"

"Earlier. It was he who told me there'd been a positive identification."

"Rory offered to take a look to spare me," Dolly said. "I didn't need anyone to spare me. Rory wasn't fifteen when his dad went off, so it was more fitting for me to take a look. It was Alasdair all right." Her tone had roughened slightly and she darted a resentful look.

"You were able to recognize him at once?" Sister Joan finished her tea.

"You mean after the face was bashed about during the storm? I was married to him, so of course I knew him. They said the body was very well preserved. I reckon it was caught in an undertow somewhere the water couldn't get. Funny things do happen sometimes. You haven't seen Rory, I suppose?"

"No. Not today anyway."

Dolly McKensie's suggestion concerning the preservation of the body was manifestly absurd. Apparently nobody had pressed her on the point.

"And at least I'll be able to get my pension," Dolly said contentedly.

"Well, if there's nothing I can do . . . ?" Suddenly she longed to leave.

"You've been very kind, Sister," Dolly McKensie said abruptly. "Makes a nice change for me to have company. Rory doesn't want to spend all his time cooped up with me. Young men don't."

"I suppose it's very quiet round here for a youngster."

"I'm thinking of selling up and going to Glasgow," Dolly said. "Once I get my pension I'll feel more free—I'll have my rights. And Rory still hankers after Morag Sinclair. I know that even though he never talks about her these days. It would be better for him to get right away and find a nice girl of his own age, someone without bad blood."

"You can't possibly mean that," Sister Joan began.

"Yes I do." The other's face looked pinched and stubborn. "Catherine Sinclair was having an affair with my husband. If there was murder done then she did it and then killed herself. I'll not have my son involved with the same family."

There was no sense in trying to argue with such prejudice. And Morag Sinclair apparently agreed with her though for different reasons. Only Rory was trapped in the middle. In the long run his going to Glasgow might be a good thing.

"I have to go. Thank you for the tea."

She was glad to be out of the flat, walking down the hill through the cool dark. Dolly McKensie was an embittered woman, unconcerned about her dead husband except where her precious pension was concerned. Sister Joan had the uncomfortable suspicion that she had seized upon her suspicions in order to justify her opposition to the relationship between her son and Catherine Sinclair's daughter. If Morag hadn't brought it to an end then Dolly would have found some way of doing so.

She crossed the road and the bridge and descended into the gully, switching on her torch briefly and then switching it off again. The moon had emerged and the stars had increased; the torchlight merely separated her from the shining of the natural world around her. Walking on to the shore, her feet now accustomed to the direction that had been unfamiliar to her only a short time before she felt as if she had melded into the dark landscape.

When someone called her name she thought at first it was her imagination. Then someone loped towards her, raising his voice as he approached.

"Don't be scared, Sister. It's only me."

"Rory, good evening. Were you coming to see me?" she asked.

"I wanted to talk to you," he said.

People talked to her all the time, she thought resignedly, and then waved her out of their lives as if the confidences they had imparted had had no effect upon her at all.

"Shall we walk along the shore for a little while?" she said. They walked in silence for a few yards. When he began talking he did so abruptly, as if the words had built up inside him and had to be expelled rapidly like pellets.

"I've decided to leave Loch Morag. Now that my father's been found there isn't any reason to go on living here. I'm nearly twenty-one, not a child. It's time I stopped dreaming about someone who doesn't care tuppence for me and made a future for myself. I can't spend the rest of my life doing odd jobs and helping my mother in the store."

"Perhaps your mother will leave too," Sister Joan suggested.

"Now that she can be sure my father's really dead? Yes, she might, but I can't hang around and wait. If I make something of my life then I can stand on equal terms with anyone."

By anyone she supposed he meant Morag Sinclair. It would be so easy to say—but Morag still cares about you. She's only avoiding you because she doesn't want to marry the son of a man who betrayed her father with an affair with her mother. It wasn't her place to say anything, however, and they crunched on over the tiny pebbles.

"I won't just leave without saying anything," he said after a moment. "That would fret my mother. No, I'll see her settled and her pension paid—find someone to help out in the shop, before I leave. Then I'll go south. I'll likely train for something, hotel work has always interested me. Morag—we thought once of opening an hotel here—extending the manse. Anyway I won't just slope off and leave my responsibilities behind."

"I hope your mother appreciates that she has a good son," Sister Joan said, unable to keep a certain dryness out of her tone.

"I hope she does leave," he said. "She never made any friends here. She always liked the city best. Sometimes I think that she and my father weren't suited at all. He was scarcely ever home, you know. I used to wish he'd stay home more often so we could do things together but we never did."

"After six years—it must still be hard to learn that he's dead."

"I wanted to see the body," Rory said. "My mother was very much against it so I didn't insist. She said it was better for me to remember him alive, but the truth is that we saw so little of him that it's quite difficult to call his face to mind. We're going to bury him in Aberdeen—a Catholic funeral. The priest there is a decent fellow. Not that I believe in any of it."

His last sentence was spoken defiantly, with a sidelong glance.

"If I were you," said Sister Joan, refusing to rise to the bait, "I wouldn't rush into anything. Talk to your mother about your plans. She may have some of her own to discuss. I certainly wish you both luck."

"You can pray for us if you like," he said with the air of one conferring a great favour.

"Thank you, I will," she responded promptly.

"Funny, isn't it?" He had stopped and was staring out across the loch. "That my father should end up finally in the water, I mean. He never liked the loch. At least he and my mother had that in common. They both preferred the city, but I daresay it suited him to have his wife here so that he could come and go at his leisure. The inspector mentioned that his body was very well preserved. That seems very strange, don't you think? After six years. Unless he's died more recently. I've thought of that too. If someone killed him—the problem is that we really don't know much about his life when he wasn't here. We don't know who his friends or his enemies were."

"Perhaps it's best not to dwell on such things," she said.

"Probably. When he was around he was quite amiable," Rory said, turning to retrace his steps. "I mean he never beat Mum or lifted his hand to me, though he could have felled us both with one hand if he'd had a mind to it. People used to tell him that he ought to have taken up tossing the caber, but he never took any interest in sports. Mum was the one who used to watch the football with me when there was a big match on television. She tries hard, Sister."

"Yes, I know," Sister Joan said.

They had reached the slopes below the retreat. Rory held out his hand, his voice suddenly shy.

"I wasn't very polite to you when we first met," he said. "I've never reckoned much to the church since I lost my faith, and I don't want to have anyone nagging me back into the fold, but you haven't tried to do that, Sister."

"Nagging people back into belief never worked anyway," she said, shaking hands cordially. "I'm sure we'll meet again before I leave, but I do wish you every good fortune. Goodnight, Rory."

When she reached the bottom of the steps she looked down and saw that he still stood there, looking out over the starlit waters. A decent young man, trying to deal with the first heartbreak of youth, she reflected, and felt glad that her first youth was behind her.

The walk had done her good, blown away the cobwebs that had threatened to spoil the clarity of her thinking. Rory McKensie wouldn't allow himself to be overwhelmed by his mother. He'd make his own way in the world. He might even find his own way back into the faith. Without nagging, she added with an inward grin.

The cave was cold and dry and dim. She switched on her torch until she had rekindled one of the candles. Her coat was much warmer than the oilskins she had borrowed. Oilskins. Now why did the very ordinary word stand out so clear and sharp in her mind? She sat down thoughtfully on the edge of the bed. Oilskins she had borrowed and worn while her own garments were drying out. They had belonged to Alasdair McKensie— Dolly had kept them, presumably because they were too good to throw out. She had kept nothing else as far as she had told Sister Joan, but she had kept the oilskins. Oilskins that had been slightly too big for her, Sister Joan recalled. They had flapped around her ankles and the sleeves had covered her hands—understandable since they had belonged to a man and she herself was small and slight.

Rory's voice echoed in her head.

"He could have felled us both if he'd a mind to it— ought to have taken up tossing the caber."

Alasdair McKensie had been a big man, much bigger than the man who had worn the oilskins she'd borrowed. Men who tossed the caber were large men, often over six feet tall and powerfully built. The oilskins ought to have been even more unsuited to her own dimensions then. And that could only mean that they had belonged to someone else—someone bigger than herself but most certainly not a prospective caber tosser. Why had Dolly McKensie lied about them?

"And why," said Sister Joan in exasperation, "don't You let me get on with my devotions instead of giving me puzzles that I can't hope to solve?"

THIRTEEN

✠ ✠ ✠

"You look tired, Sister," Brother Cuthbert said as he helped her into the boat the next morning. "You're not overdoing the penances, are you? It's none of my business, of course, but I know how easy it is to get over-enthusiastic about that kind of thing."

"Not for me," Sister Joan said ruefully. "I am more unenthusiastic about penance than you'd believe. No, I didn't sleep very well."

"I'm sorry to hear that, Sister. I'm very lucky because I can drop off anywhere, but then—"

"If you're going to remark that at my age I don't need so much sleep," she begged, "I do wish you won't."

"Sorry, Sister. I won't say one more word." He bent obediently to the oars, allowing a full minute to pass before he said, "Have you heard any more about the poor man found in the loch?"

"There's to be an inquest," she evaded. "I have to make a statement since I was the one who found him—and that reminds me—I have to explain to Morag Sinclair how I came to lose her father's boat. Oh dear, that will cost something, I'm sure."

"Money is an awful nuisance, isn't it?" he sympathized.

"Especially when you haven't got any," she sighed.

"Perhaps the Sinclairs will let me pay off bit by bit. Anyway I won't worry about it now."

"Yes, God always sorts things out," he said comfortably.

It was almost impossible to imagine on this bright, glittering morning that on the previous day the mist had been a cold white shroud enfolding the loch. Today the sun was shining brightly and motes of gold danced in the spray from the oars.

When they reached the wharf she climbed out with conscious nimbleness and waited for Brother Cuthbert to tie up the boat.

"Will you be wanting to see the abbot today?" he enquired, falling into step beside her as she started up the track.

"I—no, I don't think I'll need to trouble him. I want to finish the second painting. After that it will be a few days before both canvasses are ready for the varnish. I shall be here for mass, of course."

He nodded, gave her a cheerful wave and turned off in the direction of the beehives. She continued on past the church, past the kitchens towards the scriptorium. She would complete her work and then try to make some sense of the handwriting on the piece of paper she had found. If she could get hold of a sample that was indisputably by the abbot then at least her own curiosity would be satisfied—partly satisfied, she corrected herself, and pushed open the door.

The huge chamber was cold and sunlit, light arching down onto the illuminated manuscript with its rich colours. Her cloth covered paintings were propped up near the long table—one on the easel, the other leaning against the table leg. She picked up the latter, leaned it on the table against the wall and took off the cloth. She had been right in thinking it a good painting. There was a spring glow about it, the tiny flowers like the enamelled blooms in the margin of a Book of Hours, the church rooted in the grass like the flowering rose bush that grew against the wall. It was a happy picture, she decided, and in the same instant was gripped by something cold and fearful that caught her breath as she gazed. The little figure she had added to the picture at Brother Cuthbert's suggestion was no longer there. For a moment she wondered if by some mischance it had simply soaked into the background, but when she held the canvas up to the light that flooded through the window she saw the darker grey where someone—who, for heaven's sake?—had carefully painted the figure out, dissolving it into the church wall again. No habited figure stood, head partly turned to gaze out of the canvas, face alight with the beauty of what lay around him. The paint where the figure had been obliterated was still slightly tacky.

She put the picture down again, covered it carefully, and counted ten backwards very slowly, a remedy that she had been advised, in childhood, stopped her from losing her temper. It had never worked very well and it wasn't working now. The cold, sick feeling was giving way to hot waves of anger. Nobody had the right to meddle with the work of an artist, even if the alteration improved it. Nobody had the right to add or alter a word in a book or a poem because when that was done the original intention of the artist was twisted, something of their own individual personalities stolen away.

There was no sense in rushing out to accuse anyone. She sat down on one of the high stools placed at intervals down the length of the table and took out her sketch pad, doodling while her mind enumerated events. She had been watched when she knelt at mass, spied on while she waited in the antechamber for the abbot to arrive, watched when she knelt at the altar rail, had her hand grasped in the darkness of the crypt. Someone had hoped to frighten her away. Someone hadn't been pleased at the notion of any stranger, even a nun, being rowed over to the island. And that same person had, delicately, taking care not to spoil the whole, painted out the little monk standing in the spring sunshine outside the church.

Her pencil moved rapidly, sketching, scribbling out, doodling. She stared down at the sketch pad, catching her breath as she saw what her subconscious had produced. Was it possible? She added another touch, a light stroke of the pencil and felt the anger drain out of her, leaving only bewilderment.

At least she could do one thing. She tore out the page and crumpled it up, thrusting it deep into her pocket. Then she went purposefully to the door and out into the clear, bright air.

From the kitchen came a scent of cooking. She sniffed appreciatively and walked past, heading for the square mass of granite that housed parlour and ante-chamber. The possibility that the outer door might be locked except when visitors were expected occurred to her, but it yielded to her touch and she went in.

The parlour door was open and the small chamber empty. No fire burned in the hearth and the table was bare save for the vase of dried grasses someone had put on the table. She walked over to the window where some papers were scattered on the sill—the same notes she had seen the previous day. She took them up and leafed through them, looking for a signature, something to tell her who had written them. There was no signature. Sermons were not, after all, very often signed and these were only notes for a sermon, one probably already delivered. The actual content might tell her more.

She began to read assiduously and at the top of the third page found the reference she had feared to find.

> *To be abbot of a monastic community, dedicated to the rule, is no easy task, my brothers. I, at least, have always been too conscious of my human failings . . .*

She didn't want to read any further; she didn't want to think about that tall, aristocratic old priest rowing silently across the night dark loch and meeting the young woman with the long dark hair who went with him into the trees. The handwriting on the torn-off piece of paper in her pocket was exactly the same as the hand that had penned the notes for the abbot's sermon.

Laying the papers down on the sill again she turned to leave and gave a violent start as the abbot's eyes surveyed her from the doorway.

"Did you wish to see me, Sister?" His voice held only mild curiosity, but her cheeks burned as if she had just caught him *in flagrante delicto*—or he her.

"I have almost completed the two paintings," she said, hastily pushing the torn section of love letter with which she had been comparing the sermon notes even deeper into her pocket. "I will have to varnish them in a day or two, but after that I won't be troubling you further."

"It's no trouble, Sister. Even those brothers who regarded the comings and goings of a young religious as a dangerous infringement of the rule have been impressed by your tact so far."

Was there a faint emphasis on the last two words? She felt a guilty pang as if she were the one more at fault.

"Well, then . . ." Her voice sounded unconvincing

even to herself, but he seemed not to notice. "Back to work then. Thank you, Father Abbot."

She wasn't sure why she was thanking him save for not enquiring what she was doing in the parlour in the first place.

He gave a slight bow and she got herself out of the parlour and into the open air again without daring to glance back. What the abbot was doing was a matter for his own conscience, but when one religious broke the moral code it cast a shadow over all the rest. Her anger at having had her picture altered, her embarrassment at having been found in the parlour, gave way to a sadness as if something fine and noble had broken to pieces in her hands and revealed corruption at the core.

She walked with bent head towards the church. She had no heart to work on the second painting now. What she needed was silence and the warm reassurance of the sanctuary lamp.

In the church there was, to her dismay, no silence at all. A monk with a broom as high as himself was vigorously sweeping and cast such a look of alarm in her direction that she genuflected to the altar and hastily withdrew.

"Are you ready to leave so soon, Sister?" Brother Cuthbert came galloping up.

"I think I'll leave the final touches and the varnishing for another day," she said.

"Brother Brendan was just making some hotpot," Brother Cuthbert said. "He'll have made enough for you."

"I think I ought to go back. I must go to the manse and explain about the loss of the Sinclair boat."

"I can take you across," he said obligingly. "We just sail past the enclosure and land at the wharf on the other side. If you wait one moment—maybe two—I'll just run and get permission from Father Abbot. We usually don't go to that shore."

He went off at a run, leaving her to pick up her things from the scriptorium. She gathered them up swiftly, feeling for the first time an unease at the extreme quietness of the great chamber with all the memories of long dead monks to crowd the empty spaces. It was better to be out in the open air. When she emerged she raised her voice, glimpsing the lay brother at the kitchen window.

"I won't be staying for lunch today but thank you for making extra." If he heard her he gave no sign but merely turned away, his mouth pulled tight with disapproval. She walked on, joined by Brother Cuthbert as she neared the water's edge again.

"Father Abbot has given me leave to row to the other shore," he said. "It'll make a nice change. I've seen the terraces leading up to the big house. Makes you think of levels of prayer, doesn't it?"

"Not especially," said Sister Joan sadly. The sad disillusionment still held her in thrall, and the anger and bewilderment were both returning.

"Saint Teresa, the Spanish one, puts it awfully well, don't you think?" he was persisting. "About the four stages of prayer?"

"Yes. Yes she does." And I, she thought, am no Saint Teresa to look at the world with clear-eyed compassion.

"Lovely big house, isn't it?" her companion remarked, leaning briefly on the oars as they neared the further wharf. "When I was out in the world I often used to go round stately homes and imagine I was rich enough to buy them. I made a lot of alterations to Hampton Court Palace. It looks as if someone's coming to meet us."

The "someone" had just emerged from a car and was crossing the road to the water's edge, her long tail of dark hair bouncing against her back.

"Good morning, Sister Joan." Morag spoke briskly. "Were you coming to see me or eloping with the lad?"

"The lad is Brother Cuthbert and elopements are frowned upon," Sister Joan said, refusing to be provoked by the insolence of the younger woman's tone.

"So you were coming to see me. You too, Brother Cuthbert?"

The insolence had become teasing. Morag stood, high breasts outlined beneath her sweater, one hip thrust forward, in an attitude that made Sister Joan want to slap her.

"Meeting with an attractive young lady like yourself would be very pleasant," Brother Cuthbert said, "but I've got a girlfriend already."

"What?" Sister Joan, in the act of climbing out of the boat, almost stumbled.

"Our Blessed Lady," Brother Cuthbert said smilingly. "I've been crazy about her for years and nobody else could ever measure up. Take care, Sister. God bless to you both."

Innocence was not ignorance. She had forgotten that and felt a little pang of pity for Morag who stood, still in her pose of blatant sexuality, looking rather foolish.

"Well," she said slowly. "Well, that puts me in my place. What can I do for you, Sister?"

"It's about the boat," Sister Joan began.

"You lost it." Morag shot her an amused look. "This is a small place. I don't mix much but the tale about you has begun to rival the tales about Grace Darling and Flora MacDonald."

"Oh dear!"

"Don't worry about it," Morag said with what

sounded like genuine friendliness. "The boat isn't important. We were thinking of scrapping it anyway. And you might have done your bit in the cause of religious toleration. Even my father's parishioners are saying it was very brave of you to get to shore."

"I'll pay for the boat, of course, though it may take some time."

"No you won't. My father says that you're not to bother your head about it," Morag said energetically.

"That's extremely kind of him."

"He's a kind man." Morag hesitated, then said, "You know one of the reasons I stay here is because he really is a nice person. That's why I can't possibly let him find out that Mother was having an affair with Alasdair McKensie. Father adored her. If he ever suspected that she hadn't been faithful—let alone that her death wasn't an accident—he really wouldn't be able to take it."

"You'll have heard that Alasdair McKensie's body has been identified?"

Morag nodded, pulling the tail of hair over her shoulder and pulling at it nervously. "Have you seen Rory?" she asked abruptly.

"Yes I have. He's leaving the district, going south to do hotel training."

"Leaving?" Morag looked at her sharply. "I didn't know that. We once planned to take guests at the manse—I told you, didn't I?"

"He sees no reason to keep him here now," Sister Joan said. "I imagine that Dolly McKensie will also leave."

"The loch is dying," Morag said. "People are leaving for all kinds of reasons. Damn, damn, damn."

There was no heat in the expletives, only the heavy finality of loss. Sister Joan put a hand on her arm and spoke rapidly, before she could think better of it.

"Morag, forgive me if you think I'm interfering. Rory cares for you very much. I know he's young, but he's had to grow up fast since his father went. He can't understand why you broke off the relationship with him. He has the right to know your motives, the right to protest or to accept them. What you decide then is a shared decision. But talk to him."

"Sister Cupid, are we?" The sarcasm didn't ring quite true. "I'll think about it, Sister. D'ye want a lift round to the other side of the loch? I'm going to the village anyway. I've some stuff to post."

"Thank you." Sister Joan walked over to the car.

Morag drove carefully, probably more carefully than she usually did. Sister Joan sat silently, wondering whether she had been right to mention Rory. Other people had the right to direct their own lives but sometimes a quiet word might prevent action that would lead to unhappiness all round. She bit her lip, remembering the cowled figure vanishing into the trees with Morag. Was that an added, unconfided complication and did she have any right to mention it?

"I think that I will have a word with Rory," Morag said suddenly, her hands tight on the driving wheel. "He has the right to know after all. I don't think I'd be able to bear it if he left the district and I had to stay. It can get a bit lonely at times."

"Is that why you ride your horse up and down the shore in the late evening?" The question had blurted itself out before she could check it.

"Then it was you," Morag said.

"Me?"

"On the shore, seated against the cliff, still as a rock. I had a feeling that someone was watching us—me. It was you, wasn't it?"

"You don't have to tell me anything," Sister Joan said

and wondered wildly if there was a spiritual equivalent to "But anything you may say will be taken down and used in evidence."

"I'd be grateful if you'd keep it to yourself," Morag said. "The abbot would be terribly embarrassed if it ever got out. I mean, it isn't against the rule or anything like that . . ."

"What isn't?"

"Writing romantic novels," Morag said. "I mean, that community never makes any money and they have to pay taxes and stuff like that. And the novels are very mild—all talk and no action. It means that the brothers can go on living there, and Father Abbot can even send money to charity now and then."

"The abbot writes romantic fiction?" Whatever she had expected to hear it wasn't this.

"He doesn't type, you see," Morag said. "He writes out the first draft in longhand and brings them over to me. I edit them and type them and send them off and we share the money. We don't make a fortune but it isn't a bad way of earning a living."

"How on earth did it start?" Sister Joan demanded.

"There was a competition for a romantic short story," Morag said. "I'd just advertised my services as a typist in the local paper. The abbot got hold of a copy and sent his story to me. I edited it and typed it and he won a second prize. I went to collect it in Edinburgh. After that we decided it might be a good thing to go into partnership. He only manages a novel and a few short stories a year, and he can't very well tell one of the brothers to bring them over. The community use the letter box on the near shore of the loch but it won't fit a thick manuscript parcel, so he rows over and gives it to me."

"And you discuss them?"

"It's the only chance we get," Morag said. "There's no telephone on the island. He gives me a brief résumé of the plot and shows me any bit he's not happy about."

"In the dark?"

"I have a torch," Morag said, "and we walk into the trees, so it's not very likely that anyone would see us. Anyway usually it's only a particular passage he feels ought to be altered."

"Like the way a lover might talk to his beloved?" Sister Joan ventured.

"Honestly, the abbot never had a love affair in his life," Morag said. "The poor old duck—sorry, Sister, but he is—indulges in the odd attack of bright purple prose now and then. I mean, the dialogue has to be believable, even if the plot isn't."

"And if you both agree that a certain bit is rubbish, you tear it up?"

"Usually I just make a mental note to alter it, but the last draft had a really sick-making speech—how did you know the page had been torn up?"

"I'm a good guesser," said Sister Joan. Waves of shamed relief were sweeping through her.

"Anyway we did tear up a page in the last draft," Morag said. "Look, Sister, people might laugh if they found out or think there was something peculiar going on. You wouldn't credit what nasty minds some people have."

"I'm afraid I would," Sister Joan said, flushing.

"We don't publish under our own names," Morag said. "We call ourselves Frances Clare. The abbot took the name of Francis after some saint who is patron of writers or something."

"St. Francis de Salle."

"And he's always been interested in writing. You won't let on, will you?"

"I won't say one word," Sister Joan promised.

They had slowed down and were crawling up the village street towards the tiny post office. Outside a neat official-looking car was parked, and as Morag braked Inspector Mackintosh emerged.

"Sister Joan, just the person I've been wanting to see," he said heartily. "Miss Sinclair, isn't it? Good day to you."

"I'll get my post off." Morag reached into the back seat and lugged out a thick parcel. As she passed Sister Joan she lowered an eyelid in a conspiratorial wink.

"How can I help you, Inspector?" Sister Joan enquired.

"Your statement, Sister. I had a word with the local Coroner and he's quite willing for you simply to make a written statement about the finding of the body. The good lady at the post office has offered her back room so we can wrap up the entire matter here without having to trouble you to attend at the police station. It's a happy village that doesn't even have a local constable."

"Yes, of course."

She followed him meekly into the post office, with the languid-looking police sergeant bringing up the rear. As they squeezed past the counter into the little back room she spotted Morag busy at the counter and wanted suddenly to laugh out loud with relief and joy.

Innocence was still alive and well in the world's corruption.

At the back the room had been hastily fitted up as an office, a bag with a half finished piece of pink knitting sticking out of it pushed down the side of a two seater couch, two chairs drawn up to a table on which a typewriter had been placed ready. The police constable took a third chair near the door and took out his notebook.

"We'll just be taking the statement," Inspector Mackintosh said, and the other put the notebook away. "Now, Sister, if you'll just state your name and your usual address and then we'll take the sequence of events from the time you rowed yourself across the loch in the Sinclair boat and got caught in the storm. My constable here will type it up and when you've read and approved it then you can sign it. No speculations now—just the bare facts."

She took a seat at the table, stared thoughtfully at the sheet of paper and the pen that was laid before her and picked up the latter, pausing a moment before she began to write. It took a much shorter time than she had expected and when it was finished it looked bleak and incomplete.

"Read it over, Sister, and then as soon as it's typed you'll kindly read it over again," the inspector said. "If you agree then all you have to do is sign your name."

She read it, trying to concentrate but conscious only of the relief she still felt at the revelation that Morag Sinclair had made.

"Yes, that's all right. It happened like that," she said finally.

"We'll get it typed up then. No need for your name to appear in any paper, by the way. This isn't a front page affair."

"But surely . . .?" Over the tapping of the typewriter keys she raised her voice slightly.

"Hundreds of people disappear every year in the United Kingdom," the inspector said. "Most of them do so voluntarily. A few turn up again. Others vanish into thin air apparently, but unless there's some reason to suspect foul play they have a perfect right to disappear. Well, Mrs. McKensie will be able to obtain her pension now."

"Did you know Alasdair McKensie?" she asked.

"Never met him. This is a law-abiding place as you've probably seen for yourself, so we've no call to come out. He was a commercial traveller—away from home most of the time anyway. Ah, the typescript seems to be ready. Read it over a couple of times, Sister, and then sign it if you agree it's an accurate record."

She read it over, signed it, and laid down the pen.

"Will there be anything else?" She found it hard to believe that this signified the end of the matter.

"I'll walk with you down to the shore if you don't mind," he said. "A bit of exercise will do me a power of good. My wife's always telling me that I ought to use my legs a bit more. She's right, bless her."

"She sounds like a nice lady," Sister Joan said.

"She suits me fine and I suit her. You can't ask for more than that," he said, standing aside to let her pass ahead of him into the main post office where a plump woman glanced up briefly from a customer and lowered her head again without taking any further interest. Outside a car was just moving away. Morag sat in the passenger seat; Rory was driving. It was impossible to tell what had already passed between them, but that neither of them noticed her struck her as a very hopeful sign.

"My constable will wait in the car near the bridge," Inspector Mackintosh said, coming out behind her. "Lovely day, isn't it?"

"Lovely for a walk," she agreed, and wondered if the inspector was silly enough to imagine that she believed a lovely walk was all he had in mind.

They strode in silence down the steep street. Here and there a woman weeded a minute front garden, leaned to close a window. Sister Joan was surprised to receive the odd smile, brief and formal, but nevertheless a smile, a tacit sign of acceptance.

"You wanted to ask me some more questions, Inspector?" she said when they had left the village behind and were crossing the road to the footbridge. At their backs the police car purred gently, making her feel like someone in a spy novel being tailed.

"You know, Sister, one of the arts of my profession," he said genially, "is knowing what questions not to ask. Alasdair McKensie died of natural causes. The pathologist put in his report this morning. No marks of violence at all. Organs remarkably well preserved—heart in advanced state of degeneration so it was very likely a heart attack that killed him. He'd been kept somewhere during the last six years—a vault, a pocket of air under the loch—who knows?"

"And you're not going to make further enquires?"

They had crossed the bridge and were descending the steps at the other side.

"If it had been a case of unnatural death," the inspector said, "then it'd be a different kettle of fish. However it's clear it was a natural death and it is always possible that it was caught up somewhere. These lochs have strange underwater caves and gullies, you know. It is possible that he was taken ill, died, fell in, and was swept by the current into one of these air pockets until the storm dislodged him. It's possible."

"Did he weight himself down by the feet before he had a heart attack just so he wouldn't litter up the shore?" she enquired.

"The feet could have become entangled in all that iron. During the last war a lot of heavy metal parts got into the loch—a whole battery gun was actually dredged up about twenty years back."

"You believe that?" She stared at his broad, good-humoured face.

"The Procurator Fiscal does," he said. "He feels there is no point in making further enquiries at this stage. It won't benefit anybody, least of all the late Alasdair McKensie—and the police have their hands full with current crime without having to delve into the past where no crime is suspected at all—no murder, that is. Odd things that cannot be explained do happen now and then. Police files are full of strange coincidences, unfinished stories, you know the kind of thing."

"I've never been interested in criminology," she said truthfully.

"Living in a convent I suppose not." He was silent for a moment. When he spoke again he sounded as if he were talking to himself. "My problem is that I hate loose ends. I don't mean that I'd necessarily reopen any investigation, but I do like to know the end of a story— for my own satisfaction. Don't you, Sister?"

"Sometimes," she said cautiously.

"If the body had been hidden away for some reason that may have seemed very important at the time—it would be interesting to know about it. Well, I don't suppose we will now, unless some new evidence turns up. I'd better be turning back now. Too much walking in one day is a shock to the system. You'll be all right, climbing up to your eagle's nest?"

"I'll be fine, Inspector. Thank you for your company."

Shaking her hand briskly he said, "I said I'd not want my daughter to become a nun. The truth is there's no chance of it. She's bearing a bastard child—she and her man live in Motherwell, and they're dead against marriage. The wife and I aren't sure how to take it."

"With joy," she said promptly. "The birth of every child is a very precious thing. And who knows but the parents might change their minds and get married after all. Even if they don't it's the loving that matters."

"I reckon you're right, Sister. Goodbye again." Turning he plodded back up the steps.

There had been no love affair between the old abbot and the lovely Morag. How easy it was, and how fatal, to put the wrong construction on a series of small happenings. In a while she would smile at her own foolishness, but not yet. The truth was that she had lost her first innocent vision of the world, felt her soul tinged with cynicism. And the worst part of it was that she would never be able to apologize for the mistake she had made.

She heard the police car at the other side of the bridge start up and drive off. The inspector had left the last of the story in her hands to unravel or not as she chose. Her choice was important. It might alter many lives. The next morning she would kneel at mass. The next morning she would decide.

Beginning to toil up the pine-needled slope she wished violently that the responsibility lay on other shoulders.

FOURTEEN

✠ ✠ ✠

The sun had decided to stay for the time being at least. After the rain and mist of the previous week the world was bright and clear with only the cold snap of the breeze to hint at winter's coming. Kneeling at mass, Sister Joan wished that her spirits were as untroubled as the weather. She had spent much of the night wrestling with herself, trying to reach some conclusion that would help her to act. If she did nothing she would spend the rest of her life wondering if she ought to have spoken; if she did speak she ran the risk of landing with two left feet in someone else's life. The temptation to find a telephone and ring her prioress was very strong. Mother Dorothy would certainly advise her but telephoning during a retreat was only permissible when there was an emergency. And there were times when one must come to a decision independently and not lean like a child on the opinion of others.

Several of the parishioners had smiled at her as they walked up the track towards the church that morning. What she had taken for indifference was, after all, only shyness. Even the hostility of the other villagers might be overcome, since her having rowed herself across the loch at the height of the storm had apparently been taken as a sign that, Catholic or not, she had guts and kept a cool head in moments of danger.

223

"The mass is ended. Go in peace."

The abbot, having dismissed the Angel of the Presence, turned to enfold the small congregation in a sweeping sign of the cross. Watching the tall, aristocratic figure, she felt a ripple of guilty amusement. How could she ever have imagined for one moment that such a man would break his vow of celibacy? But then neither would it have entered her head that this man was engaged in raising funds for his community and for charity by writing the highly-coloured but intrinsically harmless love stories devoured by romantically inclined females all over the land.

He was striding down the aisle now, his acolyte scurrying ahead while a second remained to snuff the extra candles on the altar. The rest of the congregation were filing out. Through the open door the sunlight streamed, making patterns on the floor. She remained where she was and waited until the rapid beating of her heart had steadied somewhat. Then she rose and passed within the altar rail, entering the sacristy where the acolyte was tidying up, his eyes shyly averted as he saw her.

"I have leave to go down into the crypt," she said, carefully pitching her voice high enough to be audible beyond the screen that hid the community stalls from view.

The monk nodded and went on tidying.

She opened the door to the crypt and switched on the light. Going down the stone steps into the rocky tunnel she breathed in the cool, dry air. Here no shaft of sunlight entered; no worm burrowed into decaying flesh. She reached the bottom, lit the stump of candle there, and walked on into the wider chamber with its alcoves and seated figures. There was, she thought, nothing after all to fear from the dead. Whether there was anything to fear from the living she would be able to say in a few minutes. She set her candle on a ledge as the electric light went out and knelt, facing the empty alcove where the body in modern clothes had made one too many in that silent company. No words came into her mind. She simply waited.

The door that led into the enclosure proper was opening. She felt the small draught of air at her right side and a shadow joined hers across the wall.

"I've been wanting to talk to somebody," the voice said, very low.

"Why to me?" She kept her own voice low, nails digging into the palms of her hands.

"Strangers are safe, especially nuns. They don't babble like other women."

"You watched me," she said.

"Trying to decide whether talking to you would be a good thing. I even came after you into the scriptorium and stood there for a moment or two—you were in the little bathroom. I stood, plucking up courage, and then I left."

"You turned over the pages of the illuminated manuscript there."

"Did I? Yes, I believe I did. Something to occupy my hands. I wasn't fully aware of it at the time. Down here, when you first came, then I got scared. You'd poke around, find out something—I wanted to frighten you off then. I reached out and grasped your hand in the darkness—in six years nobody had counted the bodies here or noticed there was one extra. Nobody came down here save on the rarest occasions. Father Abbot discourages visits because the air ought not to be too much disturbed."

"Nor the dead," she murmured.

"Do you think I enjoyed moving him?" The whisper was suddenly savage. "I had put on a spare habit I found to make him look like the others. He had the cowl over his head. Nobody could have seen his face and the more time elapsed the more he resembled the others, but you saw the shoes. You saw those. I couldn't bring myself to remove his shoes, you see. I couldn't bring myself to do that."

"How did he die?" she asked.

"A heart attack. No violence. A simple heart attack. I could have passed by, done nothing, left her to face it alone, but I couldn't do that. Catherine was a nice woman, a good friend. She helped me when I finally made up my mind to leave Dolly."

"You didn't talk to Dolly?"

"It wouldn't have done any good. Dolly wouldn't have understood how I felt. I couldn't have explained it even to myself. All my life I was seeking something that lay just out of reach. I denied my own faith, married Dolly when she told me she was pregnant—having an affair with her, trying to prove to myself that I too could desire a woman—that wasn't fair on either of us. She was never a loving wife but then I was never a loving husband. Working away from home was a kind of compromise but it wasn't enough. I wanted to leave the world. I had what I suppose you could call a late vocation, or perhaps I'd simply denied my vocation all along. I met Catherine Sinclair by chance. My car had broken down and she gave me a lift to the nearest garage. We talked. Sitting in a shoddy little café with rain making tracks on the dirty windows. She had a lover—an English tourist she'd met briefly. He visited the area once or twice a year. That was the only time they managed to meet. His name was Adam—the surname doesn't matter since he had no relatives, nobody to report him missing—not even a job to leave. He'd a heart condition and he lived on a small legacy he'd inherited from his grandmother. She told me he was gentle, artistic, caring."

"And you confided in her."

"I'd tried to talk to a couple of priests, to tell them how I felt. They both said the same thing; the consent of both parties is required if the husband wishes to enter the religious life. I could just imagine Dolly's reaction if I told her that was what I'd wanted to do without realizing it for years. As far as she was concerned I didn't even practise my faith any longer, and I'd distanced myself from my son. She was the one who got him confirmed and all the rest of it. She was conscientious about that."

"Was Catherine Sinclair going away with her lover?" Sister Joan asked.

"No. She was meeting him down by the loch. She'd rowed across and they were on the shore at the side where the retreat is. I'd come down there for a bit to walk on the shingle, try to think things over; everything was coming to a head inside me. I knew that I'd have to tell Dolly soon how I felt, how little I cared about her—and then I heard Catherine crying. He'd collapsed on her and died. I never met him when he was alive, but in death he was slight and small. It was providence took me down on to the shore at the very moment that Catherine Sinclair's lover died. God had opened a doorway which I could vanish through."

"How? Why did it need a death?"

"Someone had to conceal the body. There might have been someone somewhere who came asking questions. In the community I would be safe, anonymous. She helped me get the body into her boat and then we rowed to the island. It was a wild, stormy night—the brothers slept peacefully in their cells. I knew about the crypt. I'd been to mass once years before, just after Rory was born, and got into conversation with the old abbot—not the present one. He told me about the bodies there."

"You brought it down into the crypt?" She imagined the darkness, the burden carried.

"There were some habits in the sacristy—neatly folded after the laundry was finished, I daresay. I took one and put it on him. But you are right to say 'it'; the body of a dead man, even a recently dead man, has lost something essential to humankind. The next morning when the community arose I was seated on the wharf with a tale of having hired a fisherman to row me across. I had a bag with necessities in it and sufficient cash to pay the dower. I gave a false name. Nobody knew me; the old abbot was long dead; it has always been the policy of this particular community to accept novices without question. I have been safe here ever since, until you came. When you arrived something told me that you'd bring trouble in your wake. I decided to talk to you, to rely on your discretion but I couldn't bring myself to do it, and I couldn't frighten you away."

"You moved the body and rowed out into the loch and sank it beneath the water," she whispered.

"I took the habit from it and wrapped it in a sheet of heavy plastic that someone had left over the wall of the enclosure and waited until I could slip away and row out a little way. It was a risk but a small one. The others were at their prayers and unlikely to emerge. One of the great benefits of the religious life is that one knows what everybody else is doing at any hour of the day. There were plenty of pieces of metal in the workshop at the back of the church. I weighted them down the trouser pockets. In the socks. I didn't want it—him to be found."

"But the freak tide came," Sister Joan said. "You can't hide things for ever."

"Yes, you can!" The voice had roughened. "Catherine Sinclair died—an accidental overdose—I didn't hear about it for a long time. Then Father Abbot, who occasionally reads a newspaper, mentioned it. I was very shocked though I hope that I concealed my feelings. She was a good friend. And now the man in the loch has been identified as me by my own wife. Dolly seized her chance. She must have known that it wasn't me even if the face was damaged in the storm. She wants me dead. My coming to life again wouldn't solve a thing."

"But she's still your wife, and she has the right to know that."

"She doesn't want to know. If she were here this moment she'd tell you to leave well alone. Alasdair McKensie is dead and buried. Let him be."

"Doesn't the other man—the man called Adam—doesn't he have the right to have his own name on his grave?" she asked soberly.

"So you're going to talk to the authorities? Yes, you're the type of woman who'd think it her duty to do that. What about my vow here? A life of celibacy, poverty and obedience would all go for nothing."

"A life based on a lie," she said, low and vehement. "You vowed first to your wife. She would probably divorce you for in civil law you must have given her grounds; you might be charged for concealing a death though perhaps they'd not press the matter; the abbot might still allow you to return here. I'll say nothing."

"But you guessed who I was. When?"

"I didn't guess," she said. "Not until you painted out the figure of the monk I'd put in my painting of the church in spring. I painted it without thinking. Afterwards I recalled that almost unconsciously I'd reproduced your face and you obliterated it. You drew my attention to it then. And your wife lent me some oilskins—she said they belonged to you, but your son mentioned later that you'd been tall and powerfully built. I think Dolly wanted to establish firmly in my mind that the man I'd seen in the loch was you—slight and small, but I think the oilskins were her own. They almost fitted me. Anything of yours would have been three times too large."

"Dolly wants me to stay dead. Nobody will derive any benefit from my coming forward and revealing my continued existence—nobody."

"That has to be your decision. We are all the keepers of our own consciences," she said softly, and waited, hearing the long-drawn-out sigh that she had heard before from the monks' stall when she had been kneeling at the altar—the sigh of a man who longs and fears to lift the burden from his soul by sharing it.

The great shadow wavered and shrank against the wall, the door closed silently, and the tiny draught died into stillness again.

After a few moments she rose, took up the candle, and went back up into the sacristy. She snuffed the candle, left it on the table where it could be replaced, and went out through the church to where the tall abbot was giving instructions about something or other to one of the monks. He turned as she emerged from the door and gave her his wintry little bow.

"Your devotions were fruitful, Sister?"

"I don't know, Father Abbot. I may never know."

"Do you wish to go on working on the pictures today? You would be most welcome."

The second painting, of the church on a winter's night, needed a few more touches before it was completed. Both ought to be varnished. Hesitating, she said, "Can one of the brothers undertake to varnish them?"

"Yes, of course."

"Then I'd prefer them to be completed by a member of the community. The second one isn't finished—the darkness isn't entire."

"My dear child," said the abbot. "It never is."

She bowed briefly and formally, wondering how much he had guessed, knowing that he would never say. Just as she would never mention that she was aware of his earning money for his community by the writing of harmless and silly romantic tales. The vow of sanctity included a delicate and mutual discretion.

"You don't wish to sign them?" He gave her an enquiring look.

"They're a gift to the community from a nun," she said, and bowed her head briefly beneath his blessing before she went to meet Brother Cuthbert.

"Have you finished the paintings, Sister?" he enquired as they climbed into the boat.

"I've done everything necessary. Someone else can varnish them. I'll still be coming over for mass on Sundays, if it's no inconvenience to pick me up."

"No inconvenience at all," he said cheerfully. "You'll be sketching other views of the loch?"

"For my own community, yes."

"I've enjoyed knowing you, Sister," he said. "It makes me feel good to know that all over the world there are people who've chosen the religious life and nobody thinks they're peculiar or medieval."

"Oh, I can be pretty peculiar in other people's eyes sometimes," she assured him.

As they reached the other shore he suddenly clapped a hand to his head with an exclamation of dismay.

"Oh dear, I must be getting peculiar myself! I completely forgot to give you this."

"What is it?" She took the envelope he held out to her.

"When I brought the boat over this morning to take you across to mass, just before you arrived, the minister—Mr. Sinclair—galloped up on a big horse and gave me the letter for you. He said to give it to you after the service, but I nearly forgot. The minister seemed an odd kind of person—very grim looking but quite pleasant spoken. Anyway I've remembered in time."

"Yes you have. Thank you." Clutching the letter she landed safely on the driest part of a small sandbank and made her way higher up the shore.

It would have been sensible—even a test of self-discipline—to wait until she had climbed up to the retreat before opening the envelope. She hesitated for about three seconds and then flung self-discipline to the autumn breeze and sat down on a large rock to read her letter.

It was fairly short, written in a bold hand with a steady pressure.

Sister Joan,

I am writing to you in the strictest confidence and I trust you to keep what I have to say private to yourself. That imposes a burden upon you for which I apologize, but even a minister of the kirk sometimes feels the need for confession.

I have never been a very sociable man, so perhaps it was a mistake for me to go in for the ministry, but I wished to serve God in the place where my ancestors had once been lairds. What I failed—no, what I refused to see was that my wife was lonely here. I adored Catherine and so I believed that we shared the same tastes. She was a good wife and a good mother, but after Morag went away to school she be-

came increasingly restless. She frequently took shopping trips to Aberdeen and spent the night away, but I was occupied with my ministry and never enquired too closely into her activities. Six years ago she went out one night—for a walk, she said. I was writing a sermon at the time and so took little notice, but when the storm came up I became a little concerned. I had promised to visit a parishioner—an old lady who was sick, so I walked over to the cottages to see her, and was hurrying back when I saw Catherine tying our boat up at the wharf. She seemed distressed, and I helped her into the house, and asked her what was wrong. She told me that she had parted from a lover. A lover? I was her husband; she had no need of lovers. I had trusted her completely and she had betrayed me with another man. I am not a man who easily reveals his feelings, and I listened with apparent calm. She had recently suffered a bad dose of influenza so it was an easy matter to persuade her to take some sleeping tablets in a hot drink before she retired. I dissolved several tablets in the drink and added a splash of whisky and handed her more tablets to take with the drink. She was completely unsuspecting. In the morning I "found" her dead— accidental death was recorded.

I have never tried to find her lover. Men are by nature weak, women are the ones who tempt them. I left him to his conscience and cleansed my own house of betrayal. Since then I have lived with my memories. I have tried to forget, but Morag grows more like her mother every day. One day she will marry and betray her husband in the same way. Rather than let that happen I would kill her with my own hands. Indeed there have been occasions recently when I have found myself devising ways and means of doing it.

I will give this letter to the monk who rows you across to the island. By the time you read it I will have suffered a fatal accident, in my car, I think. I wanted to tell one person before I leave—to make them understand that I am not doing this because I killed Catherine but in order to prevent myself from killing again.
Sincerely,
Alexander Sinclair

When she had read the letter through a second time she sat, her eyes fixed on the loch. Such a tangle of motives and actions, stretching tentacles across the years to twist emotions. She sighed deeply once or twice, then with slow deliberation tore letter and envelope into tiny, undecipherable fragments and sent them like scattered pieces of a prayer into the autumn breeze.

"So you really are leaving now?" Brother Cuthbert said, leaning on the oars of the boat. "Mind you, with the weather turning so cold it's not suitable—"

"For an elderly lady of thirty-six to stay there in the retreat for very much longer?"

"I was only teasing you, Sister. I wouldn't have said things like that to a really old lady. I had a sister once— only three years older than me, but she used to look out for me, you know. She died—cancer. I still miss her a bit. And now I've talked about my life before I entered the community and that isn't allowed—I wonder if I'll ever get the hang of it."

"Don't be too hard on yourself, Brother. You're doing very nicely," she encouraged.

"Well, I try. Father Abbot would tell you that I'm very trying. Did you know we've just sent five hundred pounds to the children in Africa? Can you imagine that—on our small income? Father Abbot works financial miracles."

"Doesn't he though?" said Sister Joan.

"It was sad about Mr. Sinclair," Brother Cuthbert said. "Fancy crashing his car off the bridge like that. We were very sorry to hear about it."

"Yes, it was a very sad accident. His daughter plans to turn the old manse into a small guest house. I think Rory McKensie is to go into partnership with her."

"He'll find her a handful," Brother Cuthbert said with a grin. "You've heard we're to be one fewer now?"

"In the community? No, I'm not on gossiping terms with the abbot."

"Brother Brendan—you'll not recall him perhaps—the lay brother who worked in the kitchen? He's been on an internal retreat for the last couple of weeks. He leaves us tomorrow—some unfinished business in the world. With so few novices entering it's a pity to lose anyone."

"I guess he'll probably find his way back if it's where he was meant to be," Sister Joan said.

"Saint Brendan the Voyager," Brother Cuthbert said musingly. "I often wondered if he chose that name because he'd been to sea, but Brother Jerome told me that he'd been a commercial traveller once. Funny old world, isn't it?"

"And sometimes a beautiful one," Sister Joan said, and raised her head to smile at the loveliness of the shining loch.